WITHDRAWN

I am Mordred

A TALE FROM CAMELOT

Nancy Springer

PHILOMEL BOOKS • NEW YORK

For oddlings everywhere.

The premise of this story was originally published in a 1995 short story entitled
"The Raven" as part of *Camelot: A Collection of Original Arthurian Stories*,
edited by Jane Yolen and published by Philomel Books. This book,
or parts thereof, may not be reproduced in any form without
permission in writing from the publisher, Philomel Books, a division of
The Putnam & Grosset Group, 200 Madison Avenue, New York, NY 10016.
Philomel Books, Reg. U.S. Pat & Tm. Off. Published simultaneously in Canada.
Printed in the United States. Book design by Gary Bernal. The text is set in Sabon.
Library of Congress Cataloging-in-Publication Data
Springer, Nancy. I am Mordred : a tale from Camelot / by Nancy Springer. p. cm.
Summary: When Mordred learns the identity of his father, he struggles with
feelings of hatred, but also fights the fate which determines that he kill the good
and gracious king. 1. Mordred (Legendary character)—Juvenile fiction. [1. Mordred
(Legendary character)—Fiction. 2. Arthur, King—Fiction. 3. Fathers and sons—
Fiction. 4. Knights and knighthood—Fiction. 5. England—Fiction.] I. Title.
PZ7.S76846Iaam 1998 [Fic]—dc21 97-39740 CIP AC ISBN 0-399-23143-9
3 5 7 9 10 8 6 4

Prologue

Because he was the King, he could show no feeling about this. The wind blew cold off the sword-gray sea, and over his crowned head the crying gulls wheeled, and at his booted feet on the black sand lay forty naked babies crying louder than the gulls. And from behind the tangle of wrack at the tide line, his men-at-arms watched silently. Because he was the King, he would not ask them to do this thing. He was only a beardless youth, but his was the head that wore the crown and his was the evil deed that had led them to this chill shore and his was the fate spiraling out of the deed and his would be the shame.

Moored to the quay, riding on the ebbing tide, waited an unmanned coracle without tiller or sail, a bare, frail, wood-and-leather shell of a boat. There was no putting it off any longer; because he was the King, he had to do this thing. He stooped, lifted two of the wailing babies from the sand, one in each arm, and walked to the quay and placed the infants gently in the boat's open wicker-floored hull.

Again he did this, and again, and again, until he lost count and the boat rode heavy with babies. Boy babies, all of them. His cloak fell back from his shoulders and he felt the cold wind cutting into him from the sea, but because of the crying of the babies and because he was the King he did not draw the cloak around himself. It was a strange, exalted, and terrible thing to be the King. Everything he did sent out echoes like a great bell. He had not understood soon enough what it was to be the King, he had thought more of being a man and no longer a boy, and he had made a serious mistake—all mortals make mistakes, but when the King made a mistake, then the sky clouded, the corn grew short, women wept, hundreds of men marched into battle. And forty babes were brought to the sea to die. Why did they all have to die? It would have been a wicked shame enough to slay the one. But Merlin had spoken: Let all male babies of the nobility born on May Day be brought to the shore. That was the sort of thing that happened when the King did wrong.

Two by two he carried the babies to the coracle. They howled, they squirmed in his arms, they squalled. The wind rose and whipped the King, the coracle, the sea; the sky clouded and wept long lashes of rain. The babes formed a pile in the belly of the coracle now, their flesh a cold pearly pink, like the insides of whelk shells. The King returned to the shore for the last two. They struggled and wailed in his arms—

No. One of them lay as still as dawn, its silky head resting in the curve of his elbow, its dark eyes gazing up at his face. He looked down at it, and its eyes, like deep pools of indigo, took him in for a moment like a spell.

That sober, dark-eyed, gazing babe. It was his. It was the one. He knew it.

He looked away, blinking out at the sea. He could show no weakness, for he was the King. He placed the dark-eyed babe gently in the coracle with the others, for he had no choice. The well-being of the realm depended on him.

He cast off the mooring of the coracle and pushed it away from the quay. It rode heavily on the salt water, swollen with babies, its leather sides bulging. The tide carried it out to sea, a little farther from land each time a wave broke on the shore. He stood on the quay and watched as the gray bobbing coracle blended into the gray rain, the sword-gray sea, until he could not tell the crying of the doomed babes from the crying of the gulls.

BOOK ONE
The White Shadow

1

WHEN I WAS A BABY, MY FATHER TRIED TO KILL ME.

I am Mordred, speaking to you from the wind with a raven's thin black tongue. I am Mordred, and it is no easier to say now than it ever was. Even hundreds of years ago, when I was human and young, when I first looked wide-eyed upon Camelot, it was hard to be who I was: Mordred, the shadow on all that shone, the bad seed.

Because I am Mordred, my father placed me naked in a coracle—a frail cockleshell of a boat—and cast me adrift on the sea.

I was too young to remember the days of starvation, the nights of cold. I do not remember my own crying. And I did not at first know that I was Mordred—and I did not at first think to hate my father, because my fishermother taught me no hatred. While she told me no lies, she kept from me the whole truth of those harsh days. Here is the way she would tell the tale to me:

"Once upon a time," she would say, "there was a poor common woman who was very unhappy."

"That was you, Mama!" I bounced in my bed until the straw rustled, for I had heard this tale many times in my six years, the true amazing tale of myself, and I loved it. She had told it to me almost every day since I could remember.

Her round brown face would crinkle with a smile as she went on, pretending I hadn't spoken. "A poor fisherman's wife. She was unhappy because her baby had died, and she had waited so long, and then to lay the poor little stranger in the ground . . . well, it was hard. The milk stung in her breasts and the tears stung in her eyes and she could not think of food or eating; she sat by the cold hearth and cried. But then—what do you think happened?"

"The fisherman found me!" I shouted.

"Shhhh. Softly, little one. Yes, it was—it was uncanny." Her smile turned rapt, and in back of her words I grew aware of the vast sea sighing and stirring and muttering like a sleeper outside our window. "Like a miracle. The good fisherman walked down to see to his nets, and there, beached almost at his door, what should he see but a fine coracle. And in the coracle what should he find but a wee naked baby boy, cold and hungry but still alive."

"That was me!"

"Yes, dear one, that was you." Now there was a bright glimmer in her smiling eyes. "The good fisherman picked you up and carried you against his chest, under his tunic to warm you, and he hurried to me—"

From his place by the fire my fisherfather grumbled, "I should have seen to the coracle first."

4

"Hush, you." Fishermother spoke gently because she knew he was teasing. He was a dank, silent man, as crusty as the salt on his nets, but she had an understanding with him. She went on with the story. "He hurried to me where I sat weeping and he gave you into my arms, poor wee babe, so weak and starved that you could barely cry, yet when I offered you the breast you suckled strongly. Like a miracle. And when he turned again to the sea the coracle was gone."

"As if it had never been."

"As if it had never been, yes. Uncanny."

My fisherfather growled, "The sea took it back, that's all."

"But the sea was calm. And never a splinter of that coracle did we see again." My fishermother spoke almost in a whisper. "Old Lyr had heard me crying, I think." Lyr was the god of the sea, who allowed Fisherfather's boat on his wide slumbering chest in the summer but shook the hut with purple storms in the cold of the year; I knew the power of Lyr. "Old Lyr had grown weary of hearing my crying and sent you to dry my tears, little one."

I lay quieted by the wonder of the story.

"Now go to sleep, Tad." My fishermother patted me. She called me Tad because I had come to her naked like a wriggling little tadpole from the sea. "Oh, look, there is the mark of Lyr's kiss!" She always made a show of discovering it, a brownish mark like an X behind my left ear. She kissed me there. "Sleep in peace."

And so I did. The murmuring of the sea was my lullaby, and my belly was full—I never went hungry. "The haddock leap into the nets," my fisherfather said sometimes in wonder. "Thank the goodliness of our blessed King Arthur." For it was the soul-honor of the King that made the fish fat and plentiful. But I did not dream of Arthur, King in Camelot, not in those periwinkle days when I was Tad. The hut was warm and the sea breathed marvels in my ear, and in my sleep I dreamed sometimes that the waves rocked me in their watery arms. I did not know myself to be bad seed cast away, and I did not think to wonder who was my real father or my real mother, for my fishermother had told me that I was a gift from Lyr. The sea was my father and my mother. And in the morning there would be warm white chowder to eat, and all day I would leap on the rocks and wade the shallows and run with the plovers on the gravel shore, and the sea was vast and the sky vast all around me, and I stood a god's gift over the sea amidst the sky, and the Forest Perilous was only a low blue mystery in the distance. And at night there would be kippered herring for supper and the warmth of Fishermother's arms and my story at bedtime, and I was happy.

It is instructive, looking back now that I am no longer mortal, instructive and curious to remember how it was to be happy.

All changed, of course, before I was strong enough or ready, on a summer day when a lady in green came riding on a great gray horse out of the Forest Perilous.

I saw her approaching, for I was gathering birds' eggs on the rocks, and as I squatted by the basket I glanced up and saw the horse shining like a mussel pearl against the darkness that was the forest. Speckled eggs dropped from my hands and cracked open at my feet. Crouching, I gawked at the horse and rider, for I had never seen such a thing, though I had heard of lords and ladies in the stories my fishermother told me. But to really see—it was beyond believing. A lady, a real lady, riding past our hut—

I left my basket and ran to tell my fishermother to come out and see.

In a moment I stood before the hut, so breathless, not from running but from wonder, that I could barely speak. But Mama was already at the door, staring.

And the lady sent the horse at a long floating trot straight toward us.

So this was a lady. I did not yet know enough to find it odd that she rode alone. She sat half sideward on the horse, and her gown flowed down like leaf-green water around her feet, covering them; I thought at first that she might not have feet, she seemed so different from my stout brown fisher-mother standing in the hut's low doorway. The lady's skin lustered as smooth and pale as moonlight. Her hair the color of a red hawk lay in sleek parted wings over her ears, then swept into plaits bound with crisscross ribbons of the same green as her shimmering gown, ending in clasps of gold. The plaits hung so long they lay like whiplashes against the horse's flanks, making it snort as it trotted toward us, a great dapple-gray horse—any horse would have seemed huge to me, for I had never seen one, but in truth this was a courser, a charger with massive shoulders and a mighty arched neck, a destrier, not a lady's gentle palfrey. My nose scarcely reached higher than the horse's knees as it halted before me.

There I stood in my coarse brown tunic, bare-legged, a child with a mouth like an O, agape at the sight of the lady upon the great gray horse, gazing up at her face—at her skin like moonlight, her eyes dark and secret, like deep pools at midnight—I looked up at her, and she looked back at me and smiled, a merry, tender smile, as if we shared a jest.

"Well met, Mordred," she said.

My fishermother wept even though Nyneve gave her a purse of gold.

That was the lady's name, Nyneve, and she was a sorceress. The snorting charger stood as still as the dapple-gray moon in the sky when she alighted and touched it on the forehead. She touched my fishermother's rough hair and said, "It is not so bad. I feel life in you; you are with child again. You will have a fine son and miss this one the less."

I did not yet understand. Nor did I understand how or why she called me Mordred, though I sensed at once that it was truly my name. Looking into Nyneve's eyes as she said it, I had recognized the name the way I recognized sharp flints under my bare feet.

"But why not leave the child here?" my fishermother cried. "They cast him away, they do not want him. No one has to know."

"But I know," Nyneve said. "And if I discovered him, so can Morgan le Fay."

I did not know who Morgan was. I knew only that a fay was a sorceress of the otherworld. I heard what Nyneve was saying, but no one had ever hurt me—or not within my memory—so I did not yet feel afraid.

I was still gazing at Nyneve. She wore no belt, but a green baldric hung from her left shoulder across her breast to her right hip, and from the baldric hung a golden dagger with a glimmering dark stone in the hilt. I had never seen such a fine dagger. Already I wanted one like it when I grew up.

"He will be safer in the castle at Lothian," Nyneve said.

My fishermother sank to her knees, weeping. But Nyneve turned to me and lifted me lightly and placed me upon the withers of the horse, amid the gray mane, which flowed heavily like rain down its neck. Then just as lightly she mounted. She gathered me onto her lap and said to my fishermother as she lifted the reins, "May the Lady, my mistress, ease your pain." And then we rode away.

I was so taken by the golden dagger and the lady and the great gray steed that I did not weep or say farewell. Also, I did not understand.

The courser surged and curvetted under us, ramping onward three times as fast as a man could walk. "Do you like to ride the horse, Mordred?" Nyneve asked me.

"Yes."

"You're a true noble." I heard a quirk in her voice as if she might laugh at me.

"I am a noble?" I asked, astonished. Though I knew I was the gift of Lyr to my fishermother, I had never thought otherwise than that I was a young churl, fit to run carefree by the sea.

"You are more than noble," she said. Her voice was soft and made me think of wild roses, as did the softness of her pale pink mouth, as did her fragrance, light and fresh and free. "You are a king's son."

9

It felt astounding at first but then fitting, that I, the gift of Lyr and sun of my fishermother's sky, was a prince. I sat taller on the horse, and Nyneve's moon-white hand curled around my narrow childish chest to restrain me.

"What king?" I demanded.

She hesitated.

"Who is my father?" It was the first time in my life that I had thought to ask.

"Softly, Mordred." Something troubled her quiet voice like wind over still water. "Softly. There are those who say you were born for ill. Those who might wish to kill you yet."

That jarred me. For a moment I struggled for breath.

"You must trust me," she said, her voice even softer. "I am one who hopes for good from you." She paused while I listened to the clashing of the horse's hooves and my own harsh breathing. Then almost in a whisper she said, "Perhaps the only one."

That night we camped in the Forest Perilous.

We rode until dark amid the twisted wych elms, the looming oaks heavy with druid vine, the black hemlocks. Up until the moment Nyneve's great gray steed carried me into the Forest Perilous, I had thought the world was made of sunshine and cloud sheen and open sky and open sea; where I lived—or where I used to live—trees grew not at all, but here they grew so thickly and so tall, oak, beech, rowan, hazel, that I could not see the sky. Something crashed away between the trees. Something cried out. Mazy trails led in all directions like tunnels, and within three strides I did not know where I was. That was the day the world closed in on me, dim and glass-green and labyrinthine, and—though I did not know it then—it was the world in which I would ride for the rest of my life. The Forest Perilous cloaked the kingdom from its stony northern shoulders down to Camelot and the sea, mantling it in shadow.

Even as a bare-legged child I wanted to be brave and good, so I shivered but said nothing. In silence I rode where Nyneve and her courser carried me.

Dim yellow sundown turned to gray twilight. In the hemlocks someone laughed. We rode on.

Twilight turned to nightfall. Swaying in some wind I couldn't even feel, a tall elm groaned like a human. Perhaps it had been something not human that had laughed also. Or perhaps an outlaw. A dead branch thudded to the ground just behind us; the horse leaped forward. Somewhere a bird barked once, then was silent. Some tendril I could not see brushed my face. I pressed against Nyneve's chest, trembling.

Nyneve stretched out one hand, and in her palm grew a flame to light the night. She held it there, yellow like a baby chick nesting in the cup of her hand, and she said, "Let us find a place to stop."

She chose a dell encircled by sighing elms. "Fire first," she said as she slipped down from her mount and lifted me down to stand wobbly legged beside her. "Help me gather wood, Mordred." She held the flame in one hand while she heaped my arms with sticks, and then she knelt and laid the

11

fire and lit it with a touch. When the campfire blazed, she closed her hand and the flame in her palm was gone. She unsaddled the horse and hobbled it, then sat by the fire and cuddled me against her side with her left arm and said, "Now be quite still, and I will cozen us some supper."

I was terrified of her, I adored her, and my awe of her made my dread of the forest seem less. Fear had worn me out, and her warmth and the warmth of the fire comforted me—or perhaps she had put a small spell on me. I lay in her embrace and dozed. I awoke only when—

I sat up and my eyes widened. I had never seen such a thing.

A peacock, a shimmering blue peacock, squatted by our campfire with its long neck stretched down, its head on the ground, its golden eyes fixed on Nyneve. The firelight gilded the great fan of its tail feathers, lifted to salute her. She left my side, bent over the bowing peacock, took it in her soft white hands and with one easy stroke cut off its head with her dagger.

She saw me gawking. "Go back to sleep, Mordred," she said, and I did so. At once.

Some time later she awakened me and gave me roast peacock to eat and sweet purple berries and mushrooms the size of bread loaves.

After we had eaten, Nyneve gave me her cloak for a blanket. Then, with no covering for herself except her green gown, she lay down on the other side of the fire from me and slept. But I could not sleep again. Night in the Forest Perilous echoed full of voices. I heard owls conversing, a fox's chuckle. The distant song of wolves. Somewhere, the dark baying of a hound—

Nyneve sprang to her feet. "To horse, Mordred, quickly!"

She tore the hobbles from the steed and vaulted onto it, hauling me up behind her, riding bareback and astraddle with her skirt flying around her knees as the charger sprang into a pounding gallop. I clung to her waist and she swayed over the horse's mane as we thundered through the Forest Perilous with the trees whipping and tearing at both of us in the darkness. I cried out, but no one heard me, for in that moment the night rang with the belling of hounds, many hounds, and the wind rose to a roar, and the trees creaked and groaned and lashed all around us as if they were no mightier than grass. The whirlwind tore the clouds, the moonlight flooded through, and I saw a great white stag leaping, leaping between the trees, its antlers shining like a golden crown. The horse stopped, or Nyneve halted it somehow by the power of her hand, and the stag surged past us, so close that I saw the flash of its wild eye white with terror. Just behind it swept a pack of black hounds like a storm cloud scudding across the ground. The stag leaped white into the black hemlocks and I saw it no more.

The hounds plunged after it, gone in the night. All the Forest Perilous seemed as still as the moonlight now, with no sound but the baying of the hounds dying away.

"I want you to remember what you have just seen," said Nyneve.

I was shaking, not only with cold. "Why?" I whispered. It was the first time I had dared to question her.

But without answering me she turned the horse and sent it walking through the night.

The dark song of the hounds sounded faintly across the wilderness, seeming to come from everywhere.

Nyneve and I rode gently in the moonlight. She had said I was a prince, but I sounded not at all like a prince as I said to her, "I want to go home." My voice quavered.

She said nothing, but reached forward and stroked the horse's mane, and under her hand the coarse hair plaited itself into a hundred fine braids, and from the tip of each braid sprang a golden bell. Then she reached back and touched her own green baldric, and it hung fringed with golden bells. As the destrier strode on, the bells spoke like angels singing, so that we rode in an enchantment made of their ringing. I could no longer hear the black hounds. Though the chill of the forest lay on my bare legs, I no longer shivered.

But amid the ringing of Nyneve's bells I seemed also to hear the ringing of the bluebells clustered around the great heavy-mossed boles of the trees. And the ringing of bluebells is an omen.

The gray horse walked through the silver night, and every stride took me farther from my home. I did not weep—already I wanted to be strong, a man, I had decided I would not cry—but I began to understand: I was never to see my fishermother again.

2

FOR FIVE YEARS I BELIEVED THAT I WAS THE SON OF KING Lothe of Lothian. Even though folk gave me sidelong looks and snickered, I did not know what else to believe.

Nyneve took me there to Lothian, a cold northern kingdom where the trees grew few and low and twisted, where goats grazed around the castle—not a castle, really, but a hill fortress, a stronghold of rough-hewn rock. On the blunt towers squatted ravens looking for dead sheep. It was a rude place, but at the time I thought it was a castle, and I did not know what I was doing there, for my awe of Nyneve kept me silent; I had not asked her.

When we came to Lothian, she did not take me to King Lothe—not at first. Instead, she led me to the chamber of the lady of the castle, Queen Morgause in a white linen wimple that hid her neck and her hair, sitting at the window with her needlework. Nyneve stood straight before her but bowed her head for a moment. Nyneve wore a peacock feather in her hawk-red hair, and her long plaits swung free. "Greetings, daughter of Igraine," Nyneve said in her wild-rose voice.

Queen Morgause looked up at her without speaking. She had a pale, smooth face that seemed to close like a soundless white door.

"My lady, surely you have not forgotten the usages of a scrying mirror," Nyneve said gently. "Do you not know why I am here?"

The Queen's dark, unblinking eyes turned to me. She did not nod or speak.

"Mordred." Nyneve beckoned me forward. "Come, give greeting. This is your lady mother."

Nyneve had left me in my rough fisherlad's garment. At the time I wondered why, feeling the chill of the stony castle on my bare legs, seeing even the serving lads garbed more grandly than I was, knowing that Nyneve could have clothed me in princely raiment with a touch of her magical hands. But now I think she was wise, for she meant my mother to take pity on me.

I trotted up and dropped to one knee, as Nyneve had instructed me to do, and I knelt very still. My mother was a great lady, Nyneve had told me; my mother was Queen Morgause, daughter of Igraine, half sister of King Arthur himself. I gazed up at her, for if such a great lady, my mother, smiled upon me, then I would stand up strong and golden and I would truly be a prince and I would forget my fishermother.

She drew back the hair behind my left ear and looked at the mark there. Then she offered me her soft white hand to touch and she gave me fair greeting. "Well come, Mordred, my son." But she did not smile.

A few moments later, in the great hall, Nyneve presented me to King Lothe. I knelt before him while he looked me over as if studying a new kind of dog, and I tried not to cringe; King Lothe was a hard gray man with battle scars on his face that showed even under his beard. I tried not to look at his left hand, for two fingers were lopped off. When he had finished scanning me, he said to Nyneve, hard and forthright as the castle stones, "Very well, we will shelter him here. And we will give him a nobleman's upbringing, for he is of noble blood. But if King Arthur wants him killed, I will not go to war for his sake."

My bare legs twitched. I began to shiver.

"It was Merlin who wanted him killed," Nyneve said quietly. "Now that Merlin is gone, Arthur will let him be."

I was in awe of Nyneve, as I have said, not even knowing that it was she who had besotted the great wizard Merlin and locked him in his tomb. And I was yet more in awe of her when I saw the anger on King Lothe's warrior face, when I saw that there was much he wished to say to her, yet he reined his wrath and said little. He said only, "Does Arthur know he is alive?"

"I shall tell him. Cherish the child well."

King Lothe, so I was later told, had been one of the five rebel kings defeated by King Arthur—and it was a hard thing to be defeated by a beardless boy-king of fifteen. But King Arthur had allowed King Lothe to keep his title and land in exchange for peace and fealty. At first Lothe had

17

used peace only to plan for more war, but now he had reason for peace: Arthur had no son, so therefore King Lothe's son Gawain, Arthur's sister's elder son, stood as heir to King Arthur's throne. King Lothe must have wondered much, when Nyneve brought me to him, whether he would be better off to cherish me, as she told him to, or kill me. But I did not know these things then.

There was a feast that night in Nyneve's honor. King Lothe sat at the center of the raised table, Nyneve at his right hand, cutting her meat daintily with her golden dagger. I sat near the end, by my mother, Queen Morgause, so that she could see to me. I wore a blue woolen tunic that she had found for me and blue breeches bound about my legs with crisscross strips of red leather, and I felt strange and grand even though they were only faded old clothes of Garet's—I had two brothers, I found, Gawain and Garet, both older than I was. Gawain was thirteen, far too much a man to take any notice of me; he sat at his father's left hand. Garet was nine, and sat beside me, glowering. There had been other children, Nyneve said, daughters, but they had died. I wondered whether Queen Morgause had cried when they died. I looked at her smooth, closed face and could not imagine her crying for anyone.

I ate little of the roast mutton with currant sauce, the baked marrows, the quail pie. I slept little that night in my fine feather bed in my own small stone chamber. In the morning I followed Nyneve out to the courtyard where her gray steed awaited her and I begged, "Take me with you."

She said only, "What was that sound?" and she looked

around. I thought at first that she was mocking me, but then she stooped, and from under a furze bush growing by the wall she drew a small white whimpering thing, soft and round, a brachet pup. She cradled it in both hands and regarded it quizzically. "Why, Mordred, this must be yours," she declared, and she gave it into my arms. "I will see you again before too many years pass. They will teach you here what it means to be a prince. Fare thee well." The white pup squirmed warm against my chest as she rode away.

So I stayed at Lothian.

That was long, long ago. Most of those days I do not remember, yet the days I do remember appear to me sharp and bright, like jewels lying in snow:

The castle cook, as I stood before her with the white pup in my arms, roaring at me to throw it into the pot—but then giving me milk for it to drink.

Garet, demanding "Is it a boy or a girl?" And me saying, "I don't know." He laughed at me and said, "Give it here," and he turned the puppy over in his hands and parted the fuzz between its back legs and said, "It's a brachet. 'Brachet' means it's a girl. You don't know anything." He handed the puppy back to me. "What will you name her?" The puppy whimpered and I said, "Gull," for the white whimpering birds of the sea, and Garet said scornfully, "What sort of a name is that?"

King Lothe—my father, or so I thought—tapping his lopped hand against his tight lips whenever he looked at me. Kneeling before him, I asked how I had come into the coracle where my fisherfather had found me, and he cuffed me on the ear and roared, "Be silent! Know your place." I cried out, and he cuffed me again, harder.

Gull, piddling on the floor of a passageway, and King Lothe stepping in it as he stood there talking to his seneschal with his foot in puppy pee, never noticing.

Garet, drubbing me as we sparred with wooden swords, taunting, "Fight, my so-called brother! You're no prince. You can't even use a sword right."

Gawain, in one of his vile stripling melancholies, teaching me letters by firelight and striking me with the ruler. "Stupid," he said, even though I read better than Garet did. "Of course you'd be stupid. Close bred." I did not understand, but Garet laughed.

Queen Morgause, giving me new clothing she had made for me, a creamy woolen tunic and breeches and a cap with a pheasant feather and a fine wool mantle with a hood. I exclaimed, "Thank you, my lady mother!" but her smooth face did not smile.

The hawks and falcons, perching blind under their splendid crested hoods in the darkened mews, like carved royalty in red and golden crowns, seeming barely alive.

Gull, no longer a pup, at my heels like a white shadow as I slipped into Gawain's chamber and put a toad in his bed.

The harper. That first winter, a harper came to Lothian; I remember nothing about him except the glory of his harp notes flying as he chanted the lays of King Arthur. It was the first time in my life I had heard music, and to me that wandering harper might as well have been the legendary Taliesin who charmed the dead back to life. The rhythm of his harp strings rang in my veins for weeks after he was gone.

Morgan le Fay.

Some things I remember quite fully even now. One of those is Morgan le Fay.

Folk said she was wicked. Assuredly she did wicked things. But I think now that she was not evil, but a bold-hearted woman bitter because there was no place for her.

My second summer at Lothian had passed. The sheep grew fat and wooly on the hillsides, blessed by the goodliness of Arthur, the flower among kings. Facing the long winter, I wished every day that Nyneve would come to see me—but instead, in late autumn, after a fine harvest, amid a great riding of retainers, came Queen Morgan le Fay, daughter of Igraine and a fearsome sorceress, to visit her sister, Queen Morgause.

Or that was her pretext. I think now that she came to have a look at me.

I will never forget. She swept into the great hall, and I stood there with a dozen serving lads, any one of whom looked more princely than I did, yet her glinting black glance darted like a starling straight to me. "Well met, Mordred!" she cried. It was like the seaside day Nyneve found me, that recognition—yet utterly unlike. Nyneve's regard had been merry and friendly and tender and sad. Morgan's gaze gloated, and made me shiver.

"Mordred, my nephew." Now Morgan le Fay's black eyes laughed, but it was a midnight laughter. "Come here, darling. Kiss me." She bent and presented her cheek. This was a favor not to be refused, so I went to her, trembling, and my lips came away from her crusty with powder. It seemed that ladies coated themselves with powder to look so pale. That surprised me; I had thought that ladies were made differently from other women. Now I saw that, without her powder, Morgan le Fay might have been mistaken for a peasant woman. She had a coarse nose, and she was older than her sister, plump and beginning to wrinkle. Yet she wore her hair in a gold net instead of a white linen wimple like Morgause's. Instead of Morgause's sober blue, Morgan wore a wine-red gown edged with gold.

Morgan le Fay's eyes glittered with life. Morgause stood like a dead person next to her.

"What a lovely brachet hound!" Morgan's glittering glance fell on Gull, and Gull crowded close to me, pressing against my legs. I bowed, backed away, and Gull and I fled.

I went to find Garet, but Garet had been put to work in the kitchen, turning a spit—I had indeed learned what it meant to be a prince in that castle, and it was this: to be silent unless asked to speak, to run errands as a page boy for the king and queen, to be as much of a servant as anyone but be bruised by swordplay and bleary-eyed with learning Latin as well. Having no desire to join Garet in the kitchen, I wandered back toward the audience hall. My fear slowed my feet. Yet I found myself fascinated by the presence of this sorceress, my aunt, Morgan le Fay.

As I reached the archway with Gull padding at my heels, I paused in the shadows to listen.

"... not a seemly woman, to my mind," King Lothe was declaring, his voice echoing harshly between the stone walls, "gadding about the kingdom without so much as a maid for escort."

Queen Morgause said something. She spoke so softly always that I could not hear her. But Morgan le Fay's words flew to me clear and saucy. "What, my lord? You think she should be home in her tower, pining for her husband?"

"I think she should be wary of meddling."

"What you must understand about Nyneve," Morgan le Fay said merrily, "is that she married Pelleas because she could have her way with him. And because she could not have Arthur; he was already taken."

They laughed. It made me sweaty and cold to hear them talking about Nyneve and laughing. I had not known she was married. Sometimes I had thought that I would marry her when I grew up; now I felt foolish and shamed. I began to edge away.

"Why should that stop her?" King Lothe growled. "She could bed him anyway and have a brat by him. Pelleas would not mind if his wife had a brat by such a mighty King."

Queen Morgause got up and ran. Toward me. My heart froze like a frightened rabbit, I froze in the shadows—and she ran past me with a face like stretched parchment; I think she did not see me at all. Her dark eyes darted, lost. I had never seen her run before, not even when Gawain was thrown from his colt onto the rocks and lay with his head bleeding.

"In druid days, not long ago," Morgan le Fay was saying coolly to King Lothe, "it was the king's right, if he came to visit you, to take your wife to his bed, and if she bore his son it was an honor and a blessing."

"Bah," King Lothe said, his voice reined the way it had been with Nyneve; he was in a rage, but he did not dare to cross a sorceress, though he bullied Morgause without fear. It must have been a great thing, if you were a woman, to be a sorceress. "You have told me this before. And I—"

"I have also told you that in olden times the most holy kings wed their own sisters."

King Lothe barked out a laugh that frightened me. I stepped back and nearly stumbled over Gull, who was quivering at my feet.

"And in the children of such unions," Morgan le Fay was saying as if King Lothe had not laughed, "the blood of the king ran doubled."

"What is your game?" King Lothe asked so fiercely that I trembled.

"Ask, rather, what is Nyneve's game in bringing him here."

"I have asked myself. Often."

"It is simple." Morgan's tone sang with glee like a skylark. "She wants to keep him away from me."

"Why?"

"There are only two things to understand about Nyneve," sang Morgan le Fay. "That she loves Arthur. And that she lives to prove Merlin wrong, even now that she has put him away."

"And you?"

"I hate Arthur, you know that." Morgan le Fay's voice became silky. "Give the boy to me."

I scooped up Gull, for her claws made more noise on the stone than my soft leather shoes did, and I ran. Just like Morgause, I ran away.

Without thinking I ran to her chamber. Her door was closed. I could hear her moving about in there and breathing raggedly. Had she been crying? I had not thought she ever cried.

She was my mother; I wanted to ask her why she had run away from Morgan le Fay and King Lothe, and I wanted her to tell me that she would not let Morgan le Fay take me away. But then she would know I had been listening. I could not tell her that, for if she told King Lothe he would beat me. With Gull in my arms I walked away.

There was no one with whom I could talk in this place where folk looked at me with knowing smiles—when they smiled. No one to comfort my fear.

After a week, Morgan le Fay rode away—without me. Perhaps King Lothe did not wish to be caught between two sorceresses. Perhaps he did not wish to give in to Morgan. Perhaps he favored Nyneve. Perhaps he planned a game of his own. I do not know, for I could not ask him.

Time went by. Another winter, deep with snow; the bard did not return to Lothian that winter. Nor did Nyneve. Another summer. Gawain turned fifteen and rode away, as was customary, for Camelot, hoping to be knighted and serve King

Arthur. After that, Garet went as sour as pickled cabbage. He would joust with me, for he usually bettered me, but he stopped studying arithmetic and letters with me. We rode out together hawking—he flew the goshawk, I the smaller birds, the merlins, the hovering kestrels—but he was a stormy stripling now and I was still a child; we seldom liked each other.

Seasons passed. Nyneve did not come again to Lothian, and I decided that she had forgotten me. Garet turned fourteen and became wild with waiting, for in another year he would go to Camelot and wear mail and fight and smite helms and proudly bear a shield blazoned with the device of Lothian: white, a quarter red, with eagles. I turned eleven, nursing a secret fear that I was unworthy to be a noble and King Lothe's son. I did not like jousting. I did not like sword fighting. Sometimes when I was sleeping restlessly I dreamed of the sea, of the white gulls wheeling and the herring flashing silver in the waves. If some miracle were to happen and I were to wake up one day no longer Mordred, Prince of Lothian, I would gladly be a fisherman on the sea. Or a bard chanting songs of old gods and heroes. Or even a sheepherder on the rocky hills, spending my days with the sun and rain and the foxes and meadowlarks. But I could tell these thoughts to no one; I was a king's son and I had to be a knight and a fighter.

Mock combat had taught me enough of fighting, so that I dreaded the time when I would have to fight in earnest; I knew I was a coward. Or so I thought until one summer day.

A hot day, so villainously hot that Gull and I were spending it lying on the floor of one of the basement storerooms. Gull was five years old then, a lovely pure white brachet, strong backed, well sprung, sturdy legged, hard of tooth and soft of temper, with the soulful eyes of a bride. When she ran, her short legs churned and her long ears flew, so that she seemed to skim the ground like a white bird. She could run as fast as any scent-hound in the pack. But this was Gull's oddity: She had not yet whelped. When she was not with me, she ran with the other castle dogs, scent-hounds and sight-hounds and harriers; she was no virgin. Like King Arthur's Queen, Guinevere, Gull was barren—so folk teased me. But I did not care if Gull never bore pups.

We lay nose to nose—I could always count on Gull for a wet, cold nose on a hot day—we sprawled on the cool dirt, and I felt so much at peace that I must have dozed; I did not hear Garet calling me or hear him stride in.

"Mor-dred!" He was in a temper. He kicked me in the ribs—this was his customary way of lifting me off the floor, with the toe of his boot—but then he did what he had not done before, what he should not have done: He kicked Gull.

She yelped, and a heat I had never felt before burned in my chest, and I lunged up, caught him around the knees, and toppled him.

He fell hard, for I had taken him by surprise. The fall knocked the breath out of him, and before he could move I pinned his arms with my shins and sat on his chest, hitting him in the face—Gull watched with her floppy ears hoisted in interest as I chastised him. I should not have been able to

27

do it—Garet stood a head taller than I and two stone heavier—but an angel of rage was in me that day. It was the day I learned to fight from the heart.

"Get off me, stinking brat!" Garet tried to jounce me off, tried to wriggle free, but I settled my knees harder on his shoulders and punched him in the eye.

"Bastard!" Garet almost wept with fury, for he was used to being the one who beat me, not the other way around. As he could not hit me with his fists, he flung words at me. "Brat, you want to know why they put you in the boat? Because you were supposed to die, stupid. That's why they put babies out to sea, to kill them when they're wrong. Like you."

"That's not true!" Till then I had been grimly silent, but now I shouted, and the shouting weakened me; Garet reared up and flung me off.

"It is true!" Garet stood facing me but he did not hit me—yet—because he knew he could hurt me more with words. "Merlin said so. You're evil born, everyone knows it. King Arthur's son and his nephew at the same time, what sort of human is that? You're a walking curse. You're the one who's going to kill King Arthur. That's why he tried to kill you. You're so vile your own father tried to kill you."

He studied with satisfaction the look on my face, then knocked me to the floor with a single blow, then strode out.

3

I LAY THERE. I DID NOT WANT TO MOVE. IF I MOVED I WOULD have to begin to comprehend what Garet had told me.

Gull padded up to me and stood over me, her silky ears hanging in my face. She whined. She licked my nose.

I sat up and took her head between my shaking hands and looked into her eyes—honey-sweet eyes, soft eyes, eyes like brown pools of sorrow—as if they were the only safe place in the world.

I saw Nyneve looking back at me.

In Gull's eyes.

Nyneve, wearing her green gown and baldric and golden dagger, her eyes sorrowful, like Gull's.

After what Garet had said, words that had struck me down like a blow from a broadsword, my first experience of scrying did not stagger me much. There was Nyneve, that was all, making my heart watery; at the sight of her I whimpered like a pup. I could not speak.

Nyneve spoke to me. I heard the words in my mind. *Courage, Mordred,* she said. *It is all true, yet it is all false. Have courage. I am coming to you.*

Courage, she said.

I needed courage, and I wanted it; I lacked it. I did not have enough courage to face King Lothe at supper. Though I felt little for him, still, to think that he was not my father after all—I could not face him or my own thoughts. I kept to my chamber.

King Arthur, my father? Every day, almost, I heard someone say *Thank the goodliness of our blessed King Arthur*— a crofter admiring the thickness of a fleece, the castle steward exclaiming over the barley crop, the cook hefting a fat capon—but if our blessed King was my father and he had tried to kill me, I hated him. I hated him. With a black flame burning in my heart I hated him.

I hated King Arthur.

But—but King Arthur was good. The people said so, the bards said so. Prince of kings, jewel of kings, flower of kings, they hailed him. If I hated King Arthur, then I must be what Garet had said, devil spawn. Evil.

I was the child of the King and his—his sister? My stomach heaved at the thought. Evil.

If good King Arthur had tried to kill me, then I must be evil.

But—if he was so good, why had he begotten me? I hated him. I hated him.

Around and around within me churned this moil of hatred

and misery. Morgause brought me chicken stew and asked me what was the matter, but I could not tell her. I could not eat the food; I gave it to Gull. I could not sleep.

In the morning, desperation gave me a sort of fledgling courage. Without permission, I took the second-best horse in the stable and rode out of Lothian gate, a skinny boy far too small atop a skewing, slewing war courser. Gull ran ahead of me, her white tail flagging gaily above the heather, and for want of any better plan I followed her southward. I did not know what urging had made me ride forth on my own. I was sure to be punished when I returned. Perhaps that was why I was doing it. Or perhaps I would not return.

The war horse carried me swiftly but fought the heavy bit at every stride. My arms ached from pulling on the reins by the time I realized where we were going: the Forest Perilous.

I had never ridden there on my own. Never so far on my own. And even when I had gone hawking or hunting with others, we had ventured only to the fringes of that wilderness. But now Gull scampered merrily into green shadow as dark as the jewel on Nyneve's dagger pommel.

"Gull! No!" One stride into that forest, I felt my cockerel courage fly away; I wanted only to be back in Lothian. I tugged my oversized steed to a head-tossing halt. "Gull!"

Out of sight in the mazy green depths, she barked.

"Gull! Come here!"

She barked again, farther away. Off to one side something gave a grunting snarl. To the other side something laughed— I did not know what.

Only fear of losing Gull could have made me go on. That,

and my brute of a horse nearly tearing the reins from my hands. With a cry of despair I leaned forward, and the war stallion leaped into the wildwood at a gallop.

"Gull!"

Just for an eye blink I glimpsed her ahead, a blur of white bobbing like a ghost in the gloom under the towering trees. Then she whisked away, gone again.

"Gull!" I sent my great blundering steed charging after her. "Gull! Bloody damn, where are you going?"

For what seemed far too long I hurtled down the meandering trails at a headlong, crashing, branch-lashing gallop, sometimes catching a glimpse of her, most often catching only twigs across my face, my chest heaving with dry sobs of fear. It seemed forever, though it could not have been more than a few minutes before—

Sunlight?

A single shaft of golden light on Gull's white flanks. There she sat, waiting for me and panting happily, in a grassy clearing.

With Nyneve.

Nyneve, her russet hair and green gown reflected in honey-dark water. Nyneve, sitting by a wide stone-walled well or pool, with Gull at her feet.

In that instant I knew that they were in some sense one and the same, Gull and Nyneve. I knew it the way I knew my name was Mordred.

Nyneve had been with me all the time—but also elsewhere.

All this I knew and saw in a heartbeat before my idiot

horse, galloping out of control, tried to run me into Nyneve's lap. I hauled on the reins and screamed but could not stop him. But Nyneve rose and laid one white hand on his head as he thundered up to her, and he stopped as still as a cloud, his halt so sudden that I nearly toppled off him. I am not sure how I got to the ground. I think Nyneve reached to catch me, but I remember only standing and clinging to her, hiding my face against her chest, trying not to cry for pity of myself—I, Mordred, so cursed my own father had tried to kill me—with her arms around me and Gull fawning at my feet.

Nyneve stroked my back, then cradled my head between her hands. "There, Mordred," she murmured, and I felt the power of her touch take the angry pain out of me, or at least lessen it enough so that I could stand straight and step back and look at her. She wore her russet hair in a thick ribboned fall down her back and her green gown gathered by a belt tooled in a spiral pattern inlaid with gold. Otherwise nothing had changed.

Only—everything had changed.

"Tell me," I begged Nyneve.

"Eat first," she said gently. She knelt by the walled pool. "For your many blessings we thank you, my Lady," she whispered as she gazed down into the water. Deep—I could see no bottom. Nyneve pulled up her flowing sleeve to bare her white arm, slipped her hand into the water and drew out a shining fish longer than my foot. She laid it on the grass where it gulped air painfully but did not flop. She reached in again and drew out another. Then she said, "Firewood,

Mordred," and when I brought her sticks she kindled the campfire with a single coaxing touch of her hands.

I unsaddled my horse and hobbled him, then sat by the fire with Gull at my side and watched Nyneve as she held portions of fish on sticks over the flames. "How did you get here?" I asked, for I saw neither horse nor any baggage. "Are you here always?"

"No. I hastened here by the sky ways and the watery ways."

"What do you mean?"

She frowned at the fire; I could see her deciding not to tell me. "Shhhh, Mordred. Eat."

We ate fish and bread. I had not thought I could eat anything ever again, but I ate the fish hungrily. That was her gift to me, warm white fish, which I had not tasted since I left my fishermother.

Igraine, my grandmother—doubly my grandmother—was married to the Duke of Tintagel, by whom she had two daughters, Morgan and Morgause. But then King Uther Pendragon saw her and coveted her beauty, so he killed the Duke and seized Igraine. By Uther Pendragon, Igraine then had a son, Arthur.

So Nyneve explained to me. "It is a hard thing to be a woman, Mordred," Nyneve told me, "and unjust." We sat on the speckled stones, looking down into the forest pool, and her voice had gone dark and glassy and very quiet, like its water. "Remember this. It will serve you."

I gazed at her, wondering if she had ever been seized by a

man against her will. The answer, though I did not yet know it, was yes.

She went on. Arthur, she said, was taken away from Igraine soon after he was born and did not know she was his mother until after he became King. Even then, he still did not know that he had half sisters. Or if anyone told him, perhaps he did not remember or take heed. He was a boy, fifteen years old, trying to prove that he was a man and the rightful Liege King. When a fair young woman, Queen Morgause of Lothian, came to Camelot, Arthur behaved as might have befitted a king of druid times.

"It is a hard thing to be a woman," I echoed Nyneve sardonically, for I, also, was trying to be a man. There I sat, eleven years old and bewildered in a wilderness, looking down into deep, dark water and not knowing half of what it meant when a man took a woman to his bed. Yes, I understood begetting. I had seen the stallions mount, had watched the mares grow round, had seen the foals born. But there was too much about human begetting that I did not yet comprehend, could not yet comprehend.

"Yes, it is," Nyneve said, keeping her voice gentle. I am sure she had wanted to wait until I was older to tell me these things. "Think of Morgause. Think of what it was like for her."

I did not think of Morgause. My thoughts were more strange as I gazed into the seemingly bottomless water. I imagined that the pool went down through the earth, ran under the Forest Perilous and joined with other waters as far away as Avalon. It seemed to me as if anything could come out of there. As Nyneve spoke, I stared at the dark water, all sheen and shadows moving—

And then I stiffened with the eeriness of what I saw. In the water. As if watching a dream, yet—I sat stark awake, and I had never seen anything in a dream so plainly as I saw Morgause, young and beautiful in a blue velvet mantle, riding a white palfrey, a golden coronet on her dark head and fear in her dark eyes, riding home from Camelot. As I watched, she stroked her palfrey's mane, and golden ribbons appeared there, winding themselves into the white hair.

She had been—like Nyneve?

What had happened?

I blinked, and Morgause was gone, and Nyneve sat there in the sunshine, talking. ". . . Merlin laid a fate upon Arthur," she was saying, "that because he had bedded his sister, his kingdom would fall to the son she bore him, and he would die at that son's hands in battle. And the child's name would be Mordred."

I. Mordred.

Nyneve looked into my face. "It is not a bad name. It means 'courageous counselor.' There is nothing evil in your name."

She was wrong. I heard dread in my name.

I, Mordred. Arthur's son. Fated to kill him.

"So he tried to kill me," I whispered.

"Merlin advised it. Arthur asked him what he should do, and Merlin . . ."

But I did not hear, for I was staring at the dark pool again, and in it I saw the gray walls of Lothian and the barley growing green and the King's emissaries riding, riding away with the infant between them—the little one lying on a shield, for not one of them wished to take the baby into his arms. I, Mordred, crying on that cold bed.

". . . you survived," said Nyneve.

I turned away from the pool and shouted at her, "I hate him!" My own passion stood me on my feet. "I hate King Arthur."

"That is spoken as a child," she said, not rising, not even angry, as if it were a small and passing matter that I hated my father. "You will grow to be a man and you will see what it is to be King Arthur. You will see why he acted as he did."

But I remembered what Morgan le Fay had said, that Nyneve was in love with him. And the hot stinging feeling filled my chest, for she had called me a child, and the fact that it was true did not make it burn any the less. I glowered at her. "I will hate him always!"

She did not lift her hands, but her scrutiny lay on me like her white hands on my shoulders. Levelly she asked me, "Do you wish to kill him?"

It was as if she had reached into me with her golden dagger and opened up my soul. I felt myself swaying where I stood, I wanted to scream, I wanted to shout at her like a child that I hated her too, but it was not true, and looking into her eyes, dark and deep as deepest water, I could speak to her only starkest truth. And that truth was: no. No, I did not want to kill this King I had never met. I did not want to kill anyone, and I did not want to be this Mordred, this fated doomster, I did not wish any of this. I wanted only to be—a person I barely remembered. Tad.

"No," I said, my voice as quiet now as hers. "I do not wish to be a murderer."

She gifted me with her tender smile. "Mordred," she said—her tone making the name an honorable one, a noble one—"good. I knew that I could hope for good from you. No child is born evil."

I felt so shaken that I had to sit down again by the pool. I felt drawn to look at the dark water once more but I resisted, looking instead at the massive trees all around me, up, up, to where there should have been sky—but the trees rose so high and so thick that instead of a sweep of sunlit blue, instead of the vast sky of the seaside that used to cup me like a god's hand, I could see only a dim and distant circle, like a dusty window in a tower.

4

"Show me King Arthur," I demanded of the pool.

The sleek water merely shimmered, a few yellow leaves floating on its black surface. It had taken me until autumn to gather courage to go back to that place—and not for fear of punishment, either. When I had ridden home to Lothian on King Lothe's second-best war horse, last time, he had met me with his harsh, angry laugh, that was all. "So you know, Mordred," he had bellowed, and he had laughed again. It was as if he considered the knowledge punishment enough. Since then, whenever he saw me, he barked out his raven laugh and turned away. Garet went about sullen and wary and let me alone. My lady mother, Queen Morgause, drifted through the castle like a wimpled ghost and would not look at me. Things were even worse for her now, I judged. For me they were both better and worse.

Better, because folk gave me a certain distance, almost respect.

Worse, because I carried my fated name all alone, and it was a heavy name for a boy not yet twelve years old to bear.

"I am Mordred," I said to the pool. "Show me my father. Show me King Arthur."

The Forest Perilous loomed around me, and the glinting water showed back to me only my own narrow young face. The pool lay all surface, like tarnished silver, not letting me in, its skin so still and taut that I could see the dimples where the floating leaves rested. I sighed and sat down on the pool's stony verge, and Gull settled at my feet as if this might take a while.

As my pony cropped the tough autumn grass, I tried to think how it had been before, this scrying. Had it required waiting? Patience? Or was I perhaps being too calm? The last time, my mind had been in a daze as Nyneve talked, so that I remembered the visions as sharply as if they were made of glittering sword-edged steel, and I remembered Nyneve's words just as sharply, but only in shards:

. . . you must understand that everything about your life depends on Merlin, on whether to believe him. And what you must understand about Merlin is that he began as a prophet, but he became a mere trickster, and he ended as a fool.

I learned some of what I know of magic from the Lady of the Lake, but most of it from Merlin. I knew him well. . . .

. . . little more than a charlatan. He would appear as a child, a beggar, an old charcoal burner, for no purpose but to make folk shudder with fear.

Think, Mordred. If fate is all-powerful, a sure doom, if no one can escape—then why did Merlin tell Arthur to kill you?

I did not know the answer to Nyneve's question.

I knew what she wanted me to think: that fate could be fought. I, also, wanted to think that.

But I had not died when my father tried to fight fate by killing me. Had fate saved me?

My father. Had he felt as trapped in fate as I did now?

"My father," I whispered to the dark pool. "Show me King Arthur."

Trees rustled. The surface of the pool did not ripple, but deep in the still water, shadows swirled. It was happening. I made myself be as still as the pool, calm, not blinking, barely breathing. I waited.

And then I saw.

My father, King Arthur? No.

All I saw was Nyneve.

As plainly as if I watched her through a glassed window, there she was, Nyneve, seated at her ease in a pleasant solarium, her green silk gown bordered with gold. On a small table before her stood a golden goblet. Beside her at the table sat a tall man with a gentle, handsome face, and on his mantled shoulder perched a milk-white falcon. The man—the knight, for he had the bearing of a noble—gazed at Nyneve with love like sunlight in his eyes as she reached for the goblet, and drank, and set it down again, and smiled on him.

"Nyneve," I whispered, my heart turning to water as always when I saw her. Then it was as if in the vision I drew closer, somehow, although I sat by the pool and had not moved. As if I had tapped her on the shoulder, Nyneve turned.

"Why, Mordred!" Her dark eyes gazed straight into mine as she gifted me with her merriest smile. "Your mother's blood runs strong in you. When did you learn scrying?"

I could not answer. My heart was beating hot at the sight of her sitting there with that handsome knight, and I felt all too much the child. I whispered, "Where are you?"

"Caer Avalon. My home. With my husband. Is something wrong, Mordred? You wish to speak with me?"

I shook my head. "I wished—I asked to see King Arthur."

"Ah." Her smile grew softer, as if to say, *I see*. But instead she said, "Why?"

"I—I don't know." I was hoping for something, but not sure what. Hoping that if I saw him, if I looked into his kingly face, I would find some knowledge, some certainty, some measure of peace.

"If you want to scry King Arthur, try a mirror, Mordred," said Nyneve wryly. "The pool will not show him to you."

I stiffened, because her tone condescended to me, as if I should have known this already. "Why not?"

"I will show you. Take the water in your hands."

"But—" But that would ripple the surface, and surely I would lose sight of her.

"It will be all right, Mordred. Go ahead. Touch the water."

I had touched it before. I had washed in it, the last time, and it was just water like any other water. Nevertheless, because Nyneve told me to, I bent over the pool and cupped a splash of water between my two hands. It sparkled like quicksilver for a moment, then trickled away—but in that moment, I felt a presence wash through me or around me as big as the world, and for no reason I thought of a warm brown woman I had almost forgotten: my fishermother.

Ripples spread and faded. Once again the water lay dark and still. I could not see Nyneve.

Yet somehow she spoke to me. Within my mind. *It is motherwater,* Nyneve told me softly. *The very tears of the Lady. It will show you only what is good for you to know.*

I stood up and walked to my pony, my back straight and hard as a sword. I left that place.

"My lady." As befitted a humble page boy, I dropped to one knee before Queen Morgause. I never called her Mother; that word was for Gawain and Garet to say. When Garet ran to her, her smooth face softened into a smile, her dark eyes shone. But looking on me, her eyes went as dull as pebbles.

Gull pressed warm against my leg as I said to Queen Morgause, "I would like to beg a boon, my lady."

She sat at her chamber window with her needlework in her hands but her hands slack in her lap. Her face, turned to me, looked as blank as her head linen and nearly as pale. She had grown even more silent and white since Garet had let the secret out like letting a devil loose to fly in the air of Lothian. Now King Lothe found me a sour jest, the sight of me puckered his mouth like pickled sweets. Now all his temper was for her.

Knowing what it meant to be Mordred troubled me so

much that it made me bolder. I had never before dared to beg a boon of her.

"My lady?"

"Speak."

"My lady, teach me the ways of—" I did not want to say the word *scrying*. Magic of any kind was secret, forbidden, dangerous. But my wish to see King Arthur had hardened from whim into resolve, and if the pool would not show him to me, well, then . . . There was only one mirror in Lothian castle, my mother's dressing mirror of polished silver, and the few times I had been able to look into it, it showed back to me only my own thin young face, my beardless cheeks still childishly soft. I did not know how to see otherways in a mirror. I said, "My lady, teach me the way of seeing, in a mirror, that which is far away."

Her pebble eyes turned to flint, hard and sharp. "How dare you."

Danger. I had overstepped. But how? What had I said? "I beg pardon, my lady." I lowered my head.

"You are the reason my life is ruined. What, would you destroy it anew now?" She did not raise her voice, but it had gone as raw as a scraped knee. She cuffed me, but she did not know how to hit hard; her ragged, bleeding voice hurt me more than the blow. I do not know whether her white face curled in hatred of me; I did not dare to look at her. "Begone," she commanded, and I rose to my feet and fled, with Gull scampering after me.

Destroy her life anew? What did she mean? What I wanted to see—how could that hurt her?

44

I wanted to see my father. King Arthur. That was all.

I wanted to see his face.

I wanted to see whether he was as kingly as the bards claimed. I wanted to see whether I resembled him in any way.

I wanted to see whether he looked worthy of my hatred.

The moon swelled yellow. Once again the harvest was plentiful, putting flour in the barrels, apples in the bin. *Bless the goodliness of our liege King Arthur.*

Shortly after the harvest, splendid in red satin and riding at the head of a shining entourage, came Morgan le Fay once more to visit her sister.

Once again she fussed over me, presenting to me her powdered cheek to kiss, but this time her attentions did not end there. All through dinner I felt her glittering gaze on me, while King Lothe roared with raven laughter at the head of the table and Queen Morgause sat like a white wraith at the foot.

After the meal, Morgan le Fay rustled up to me. "Such a pretty brachet," she cooed, bending with one hand outstretched; Gull shrank back.

"Yes." My voice came out a whisper, for it frightened me that she noticed Gull—even though Gull was just a dog, as Nyneve had made quite clear to me. Gull could not speak to me, or reason with me, or advise me as Nyneve did. Nor did Nyneve spy on me through Gull's eyes or know what I was doing. This she swore. It was only that—in Gull, Nyneve was with me. Her warmth, her merriness, her constancy, her happiness when I was well, her sorrow when I was sad. Her soul.

"Will you walk her now? It is a lovely night. I will come with you."

A lovely night? It was cold, silvered by moonlight and icy as a witch's fingers, or so I felt it—I have never taken kindly to cold. But Morgan le Fay walked out bareheaded with Gull and me. The castle gate hung open day and night, such was the peace of King Arthur's reign. Morgan le Fay and I walked past bored guards to the furzy common where Gull trotted away from us.

"Mordred," my aunt, the sorceress, said to me—and she had dropped her cooing tone—"tell me what is going on."

Silently I begged Gull to be quick. "I—I beg your pardon, my lady?"

"It is no secret to me that King Lothe has long since ceased to love your mother," Morgan le Fay said, "but something more has happened between them to make her so pale. What is it? Tell me."

Her eyes glittered even in the dark. She did not pretend to be concerned; she simply and willfully wanted to know. Yet, even though I knew I should fear her as a sorceress, her matter-of-fact tone made me able to speak to her almost as an equal.

"I don't know," I said. "It is because of me, I think."

She chuckled, standing there looking hard as glass in the moonlight. "It has always been because of you, Mordred." There was no pity in her, yet it eased me to hear her say this, to know that I was not a child for thinking so. "Because

46

you were born and did not have the grace to die." As Gull came scampering up to me, white like a good ghost in the dark, Morgan le Fay went on, "But something has changed, has it not?"

Gull's sober gaze made me think of the pool in the Forest Perilous, and of Nyneve, and made me feel how far I must stay from speaking of them to my aunt, to anyone. But I had to answer something. I said, "I asked my mother to show me how to scry in a mirror." Some instinct made me say "scry" boldly to Morgan le Fay; daring was less dangerous than cringing in front of her.

"Why, Mordred!" She laughed, much diverted. "Scrying is for women, don't you know that? She would not show you, would she?" My silence answered her. "I thought not." She laughed anew. "What do you want to find out, Mordred? What did you want to see?"

Because her laughter stiffened my spine, I answered boldly again. "I want to see my father. King Arthur."

She laughed again, but this time low and dark. I shivered, remembering the dark voices of the black hounds in the night of the Forest Perilous. She stood regarding me with glinting interest.

"I will teach you how to scry," she said, and something had put teeth in her tone.

She asked no more questions of me. I think that by saying my father's name I had answered all her questions. Or else she saw more to be gained.

"Come," she said with hard-edged sweetness, "is your bitch quite finished? Let us go within."

She took me to her chamber—I barely recognized the place as Lothian, for it seemed that Morgan le Fay journeyed nowhere without a great many draperies; tapestries hung everywhere, masking the stone. I stared at them, at twisted beasts stitched in thread of gold, but Morgan le Fay brushed past them and ordered her maidservant to find her a mirror. The girl brought her a circle of polished metal from her baggage—bronze, or perhaps brass. I had thought that Morgan le Fay would have a silver mirror with a tooled border, like Queen Morgause. Perhaps this one was her second best, for traveling. She took it by its handle from the maid, sent her out of the room with a gesture and closed the door.

"Your mother," she said to me with a quirk in her voice, "was afraid that you would see the seduction."

She blew out the candles, then placed the mirror on the floor, where it lay like a small pool, shimmering in the moonlight that sifted into the room through the high, narrow windows.

"A moonless night would be better," Morgan le Fay said. "But it is dark enough." She settled herself on the bed—the ropes creaked under her weight, and the canopy shifted. "Sit on the floor, Mordred, and look slantwise in the mirror. Think of what you desire to see and let the desire fill you. Then be still and gaze without blinking until you see nothing that is in this room."

I could not have seen my own bony face in the mirror if I tried. That small circle of metal lay like a mystery, all shadows and intimations. I stared, and lost sense of time, and the shadows began to swirl, and in the shifting dimness I saw the sheen of gold—and then—it was he, King Arthur, I knew it by the coiled druid vine work of his crown. He stood with his back to me, on some lonely shore, staring out to sea. I saw his wine-red cloak, his broad shoulders, his curling hair nearly as golden as his crown, and in a moment he would turn, my father, I would see more, I would see—his face—

But as if feeling a cold shadow fall upon me I felt the presence of Morgan le Fay in the room with me; could she see what I was seeing?

I did not know. There was too much I did not know about her. Where did she live? How did she come to travel like a queen? Where were her husband, her children? Did she have none? Had she killed them?

That thought came out of nowhere. It made me blink, and the vision of my father, King Arthur, vanished before he could turn his face to me.

Stiffly I struggled to my feet. "What did you see?" asked Morgan le Fay.

"Nothing, my lady. I saw nothing." My heart was a white stag leaping in my chest; I would share nothing of my father with her. "I—I am weary, my lady. By your leave." I bowed to her and bolted, running to my chamber.

My dreams that night were of Arthur, King Arthur, Very King, looking out to sea.

The sea. I only dimly remembered the sea, but those up-reaching waves were all entwined with my memories of my fishermother, warm white soup, the little hut under the wide bright sky. Perhaps it was because I had seen my father by the sea that I began to have bright dreams of him. Or per-

49

haps, in a backward way, it was because of Morgan le Fay. I thought about her much, and what I chiefly thought was that Morgan le Fay had taught me scrying for a reason. What did she hope I would see? My father embracing my mother? My father placing me, an infant, in the boat where I was meant to die?

She wanted something of me.

The morning she left, I awoke to find on my chamber floor a small, muslin-wrapped packet that had been slipped under the door. I opened it and found the brazen mirror.

When I stood with my mother and brothers at the gates to see her off, she smiled upon me with some hard knowledge in her glittering eyes.

She wanted something. And whatever it was, I did not want to give it to her.

From time to time after she left I tried scrying, sitting cross-legged on my chamber floor in the darkness and gazing slantwise at the circle of brass. But I saw only hints and cloudy shapes, like a gathering storm. Once I saw black wings, and once I saw a white falcon flying hard against the wind. I did not see King Arthur again. I think I did not want to see him first in this round of yellow metal. I did not trust it. After a while I stopped looking in it; I would dream my own dreams.

Time passed. Garet turned fifteen years old and rode away toward Camelot with excitement reddening his cheeks. In a few years it would be my turn to serve King Arthur. Meanwhile I was much alone. Days, I went about my tasks and my lessons. At night, warm in my bed and not yet quite sleeping, with Gull curled by my chest, I dreamed.

In the dreams I was a knight of the Round Table, defending King Arthur's honor and spreading his fame. In daylight and in fact I loathed fighting, but at night, in my dreams, I was King Arthur's mightiest champion. When he was unhorsed in battle I slew the opponent riding the finest steed and presented it to my liege. He gave me a quest for a magical sword or an enchanted cauldron, something important, and I brought it back to him—no, wait, I was wounded in my side, and fell down in a faint, and he healed me with his tears and the touch of his hands. I was the fairest knight of his Round Table, purer than Sir Galahad, more valorous than Sir Lancelot. But no, wait—I was not just his knight. I was his son. My father, King Arthur, had no other son—for almost as many years as I had been alive, Queen Guinevere had failed to bear him a son or a daughter. Would he not be glad to have me now, would he not welcome me to Camelot as his son and his prince? When I rode to Camelot, King Arthur would ride out to meet me on a white charger, he would stop his horse next to mine and reach across the small distance between us and embrace me. Before a gathering of all his lords and barons he would place a princely crown on me with his own hands. I could be a good prince, I knew I could, if my father loved me; I had almost forgotten that I had ever hated him. Guinevere would be jealous of his love for me but I would be kind to her. I would be gallant and wise. And when my father, King Arthur, died, I would rule the kingdom and the people would call down blessings on me: *Bless the goodliness of our liege King Mordred.*

King Arthur, prince of kings, jewel of kings, lily and rose of kings—I was his son. My heart fluttered like linnet wings at the thought; it warmed me in the long, cold winters of Lothian. I was his son; surely he would acknowledge me; surely there was Princeliness in me.

As if hanging on a slender chain of gold, my life waited for the day when I would ride into Camelot, for the moment when I would first look upon his face.

BOOK TWO

The White Stag

5

C AMELOT.

Out of the Forest Perilous at last, blinking as shadows gave way to sunlight, I halted my horse to stare. Gull lay down like a nesting bird beside me, and the four retainers at my back halted, not even grumbling as I gazed. Across a rising sweep of green meadow, there it stood, the flower of castles, tower above tower above outer wall and inner wall and barbican and bastions and keep, as mighty as if it had grown out of the bones of earth, as if the stone giants had raised it there, but—shining white. Not stony gray but white, like cloud froth, sea spray. Camelot aspired so mighty yet so water-lily white in the morning sunlight that I clutched the reins and could not speak.

One of my retainers said gruffly, "Well, lad, ye've done it." They had depended on me to guide us there, all the monthlong way from Lothian, for Camelot is a castle under a spell; one cannot find it by maps or ordinary means. It will welcome no one who is not meant to be there. I said nothing, for my heart began to pound with doubt; it was not I who had brought us through the Forest Perilous to Camelot, but Gull. All I had done was follow her.

Still, I would ride up the grassy rise to Camelot. I would ride in and find my father, upon whose welcome the course of my life depended. I could not do otherwise.

I swallowed hard and took breath to order us forward, but at that moment I heard a merry clamor of bugles and laughter, the great gates roared open, and I gazed anew as a bright cavalcade spilled out of that white castle. I saw green caps, red and blue cloaks thrown back, lords and ladies cantering in happy confusion on pleasure horses streaming with silken trappings, white and blue and gold. Then I knew that this was the morning of May Day, and the nobles of Camelot were going a-Maying.

My fifteenth birthday. I would meet my father today.

The thought made me feel as thin as water, as if I could not support the slight weight of my chain mail, my plain leather helm, the short sword hanging at my side. I should have waited. King Arthur would look at me and know I was not yet worthy to be a knight, far less his son and a prince. When he was my age he was already King, not a stripling in a leather helm. I should have waited, and perhaps King Lothe would have given me a metal helm, a broadsword, and a shield. But King Lothe had shouted at Morgause and gone somewhere; he not been there to make me stay.

And I had ridden off to Camelot. To kneel before my father. King Arthur.

If I kept thinking about it I would begin to shake. I pressed my lips together and lifted the reins. "Forward," I said, my voice not as steady as I would have liked.

I sent my horse jogging up the meadow with my escort at my back. Riding across a wide sweep of rippling grass under an open sky was almost like being back to the sea again. A green sea that rose to a white crest: Camelot.

The nobles in their laughing cavalcade rode nowhere near me, but more toward the south; no one should have seen me watching from the edge of the Forest Perilous. But even before I sent my horse into the open, two riders veered away from the others and cantered straight toward me.

On a golden mare, a slim maiden in a green gown, her long hawk-red hair flying. Riding beside her, a handsome knight with a white falcon gliding above him.

I pulled my horse to a halt again and could not move. Gull ran forward, barking gladly.

"Nyneve," I whispered.

My voice came out such a croak that she could not possibly have heard me—but it did not matter. She cantered up to me, halted her horse beside mine, leaned toward me and hugged me as if I were still a child. My heart went so hot that I did not dare to embrace her in return. I could only stare at her.

I had not seen her in four years, yet she looked just the same. Except for the wisdom in her smiling eyes, she might have been a girl of nineteen. Her husband, though, Pelleas—there were lines around his eyes and threads of silver in his hair and beard since I had last seen him, since that time I had tried scrying in ladywater.

When I had been a child, Nyneve had seemed like a fair

and fearsome lady to me; now she seemed nearer my own age. "You're getting younger," I blurted.

She laughed—her laugh always reminded me of the rich ringing of bells. "No, I am staying the same," she declared. "You are getting older. Well come, Mordred!"

"You knew I was—"

"Yes. That is why I am here." She turned her horse, and at a gentle walk we rode toward Camelot. Pelleas rode at my other side, and I did not know what to say to him. I glanced at him, and he smiled at me. His eyes were kind.

"Court bores me, usually," Nyneve added.

Gull frisked ahead of us, nine years old but still as playful as a puppy. The white falcon swooped low over her, and my heart beat like wings as I watched—it did so every time I saw a falcon fly. Thought is not as swift. Falcons whip through the air, their pointed wings blur with speed, they scorn slow game such as hares, they prey on songbirds on the wing. They scud high and drop like stones, like thunderbolts, they strike so hard that a dove becomes a puff of feathers floating to the earth like snow. Pelleas's falcon was small and probably fed mostly on sparrows, but if she wanted to, she could kill birds twice her size.

With her pointed tail spread handsomely, the white falcon swooped over Gull, and Gull leaped, her long ears flying, as if she wanted to join it.

I felt the prickle of an uncanny knowing in my bones. "Both of them," I whispered. They were both Nyneve; I knew it quite surely, but I did not know how to say it or whether I should.

"Yes," said Nyneve as placidly as if we spoke of the weather, "in them I stay with you, and with Pelleas, even when I must be away from you."

"You are honored, Mordred." Pelleas spoke to me for the first time, his voice deep and warm.

"But—are there—no others?" My thoughts veered to the white stag I had seen leaping for its life in the Forest Perilous, with the black hounds scudding at its heels.

Nyneve laughed her golden laugh again. "Have mercy, Mordred! How much do you think I can do?"

"No others," Pelleas told me. "Just the brachet for you. And the falcon for me."

"Then I am indeed honored."

I was not to meet King Arthur that day. He had gone somewhere by himself, Nyneve said. Always on May Day he went off by himself and returned late and somber. Wait a day, she advised.

"Does he know I am here?"

"He knew you were on the way."

"You told him?"

"Yes."

I leaned back in my chair and stared at her. She and Pelleas had sent my men to the barracks and led me to their lodging. They had an entire tower to themselves—a fair, airy place with silk oriflammes hung on the whitewashed stone, brighter than any tower of Lothian would ever be. And more hospitable. Nyneve and Pelleas themselves had helped me take off my mail and helm and sword and heavy boots. They had ordered me a warm bath scented with rose petals and they had given me a velvet robe and soft buskins to wear. In the sunny top room, we sat on soft chairs almost like thrones while a servant brought wine.

"What did he say?"

"He said he would not prevent you."

It was not what I wanted of my father, the King. I tried again. "What about years ago? When you first took me to Lothian, you said you would tell King Arthur I was alive. What did he say then?"

Under the table Gull lay gnawing a meaty bone the servant had brought her from the kitchen; I felt her press warm against my feet. On Pelleas's shoulder, the falcon fluffed her milky feathers, clacked her beak, and turned her golden-eyed gaze on me. A falcon's eyes are set on the front of the head, like a person's; her regard felt nearly human, though fierce. I liked seeing her perching there unleashed and un-hooded, able to fly if she chose, able to look at me.

Nyneve was looking at me also, but not so fiercely. "He said nothing. He is the King; he cannot always speak what he is feeling. He was glad, I think." She paused to consider. "And afraid. Mordred, you must understand how noble he is. He believes what Merlin foretold, yet he will greet you with courtesy."

I wanted far more than courtesy from him; I became sulky to hear her speak of him so warmly. Also, I had drunk wine, and I was not accustomed to it. Some childish urging made me say to her, "Morgan le Fay says you love him."

If I was hoping for a blush from her or a jealous growl

from Pelleas, I got neither. Sitting beside her, across the table from me, Pelleas glanced at her with a smile. And she smiled just as merrily at me.

"I do, indeed; how could I not love him?" Then she rolled her eyes. "Though not as Morgan would like to think."

"I thank King Arthur's goodliness that Nyneve is alive and mine today," Sir Pelleas said to me.

His quiet words made me feel how young I was, a spoiled child when they were treating me as their honored guest, a spiteful child trying to make trouble between them. I pushed my wine goblet away. "He gave her to you?"

Now that I did not mean to anger him, yet I saw him flush and scowl. "No one owns her to give her to me or anyone."

The falcon moved, pressing warm against the side of his head. Nyneve touched his hand.

"I beg pardon," I said.

"No harm," Nyneve told me. "You speak no more ignorantly than most men. King Lothe, for instance. Or that ruffian Sir Outelake."

It was not a name I had heard before. "Sir Outelake?"

Sir Pelleas sat back, and Nyneve told me her story.

It began as one of Merlin's tricks—though Nyneve did not know Merlin then. Fostered by the Lady of the Lake, she was fourteen years old, barely a woman, when Merlin laid his mischief on her. Perhaps he sensed a rival in her, though she did not yet know her own power. Or perhaps his own strange fate made him do it. For whatever reason, he chose her from afar to be his victim.

"I was riding a little nodding donkey of a palfrey," Nyneve said, "when I heard a baying like the hounds of the horned god of the dead, and here came the white stag running for its life with thirty pairs of black hounds yelping close behind it. And my white brachet—it should never have happened, but she ran away from me to hunt it with them."

Nyneve knew that I would understand: The brachet was she, herself, being cozened against her will. Merlin had stolen her soul and turned it into a beast that hunted blood. She galloped in pursuit, running her little palfrey wild with fright through the Forest Perilous, and the hunt swept her straight to Camelot and right into the great hall where young King Arthur sat feasting with his knights. She saw him watch openmouthed as the white stag leaped the table before him. She saw her ensorcelled brachet tear at the stag, opening a bloody wound. She saw a knight take the brachet and run away with it as the stag doubled back and darted out the door.

Sobbing, she cried out to the King, "Summon the knight who has stolen my brachet!"

But then, as Merlin smirked beside the astounded King on the dais, a fully armed knight rode into the great hall and seized her.

"He carried me off and paid no heed to my screaming," Nyneve said. "To him I was nothing more than a haunch of meat he fancied, not yet dead."

The knight was Sir Outelake. He carried her away and made it clear to her that she was his chattel, his property, just as if she were his horse or his cow, and he would have done to her what he liked except that King Arthur sent one of his knights after her.

"Was that you?" I asked Pelleas.

He shook his head. "No," Nyneve said with a quirk in her voice, "I met Pelleas later. No, I am grateful to Arthur, but I was in almost as much danger from the knight he sent as I was with Outelake. It was Pellinore."

I did not then understand about Sir Pellinore, and Nyneve did not tell me. She went on to explain that Pellinore fought Outelake, not because Outelake had seized her against her will, but because Outelake claimed he had taken her by force of arms and Pellinore knew that he had not. Also because Outelake angered him by killing his horse. Fighting afoot, Pellinore killed Outelake with a single blow.

"He took me straight back to Camelot because Arthur had told him to do so," Nyneve said. "That, I think, was the only reason. And King Arthur restored my brachet to me. It is for his good heart that I love him. And that day I swore to myself that I would learn sorcery, and that I would never be owned by any man."

I heard voices and laughter outside and stood to look down on the courtyard from the tower window. Through the great white arch of the castle gate, the nobles who had gone a-Maying were returning, their heads garlanded with primrose and buttercups, daisies twined in their horses' manes. I would have liked to have gone a-Maying with some damsel as fair as Nyneve.

"When I met Pelleas," said Nyneve more softly, "I saw that he knew how to love a woman truly."

The horses were all frivolous colors—piebald, trout-speckled gray, star-spotted, blue roan, strawberry dun; I saw a golden chestnut with a silver tail and mane. I looked at the horses, the flowers, the noble knights and ladies, not at Pelleas and Nyneve. After a moment Nyneve rose and came to stand by my side, looking out of the window with me. "The tall damsel in the purple mantle," she said, "is Queen Guinevere."

I looked again and saw her golden crown almost hidden under the masses of cowslip and columbine in her honey-brown hair. Guinevere was plain faced, but regal, and graceful in all her movements, and everything about her made me think of honey; she had a golden sheen of sweetness.

I saw her smile and lean close to a tall knight who followed by her side, her lips at his ear, whispering to him, and I asked Nyneve, "The one with her—that is not King Arthur?"

Nyneve often laughed at me, as I have said—though never when it would have hurt me—but she did not laugh now. She said merely, "No. That is Sir Lancelot."

I gazed down on Queen Guinevere and wondered why she did not bear sons for King Arthur, and why he did not put her away from him and take another. And I wondered where he was.

I found Gawain and Garet sharing a small chamber on the ground floor, close to the barracks. It did not surprise me that their lodgings were modest. What surprised me was that they greeted me as a brother.

"Mordred! Well come!" Gawain strode to me and hugged

me like a great ruddy-haired bear, which he resembled. He had grown; he was a burly, bearded man now. But what changed him most was the light in his eyes. He was happy.

"Still followed by the same white shadow, Mordred?" Garet patted Gull. Still a young knight, he had not changed so greatly, yet a happiness like Gawain's lighted his face as well. "How old is that dog now?" He did not wait for an answer. "Come in, sit down!" He sat on his cot for want of a third chair. "Why did you not send word? We would have had a bed ready for you. We were not expecting you until midsummer."

"I came on my own."

"Couldn't wait, eh?" That was Gawain, with a warm laugh. "Good. You'll be glad you came."

I studied both of them curiously as we talked; they asked for news of Lothian, their father, our mother, but seemed unconcerned with what I told them, as if they planned never to go back there. "You like it here," I said after a while.

Gawain turned to me with his smile quieting into a rapt look, his mouth faltering as if he could not find words. "Arthur truly is a good King," he said at last.

"A great King," said Garet with the same grave rapture. "We are blessed and honored to serve such a King."

"My father." The words winged from me before I could think to stop them.

Gawain leaped to his feet. "Do not say that!" He loomed over me, though not as if to threaten me; he seemed frightened. His face tightened almost as if he might weep. "Never say that. Who told you that?"

Beyond him I could see Garet standing with his hands

fumbling, his face pale; I did not answer the question. "Why should I not say what all the world knows?" I asked, staying where I was, in my chair, keeping my voice level and low. Then, because they were only my lunkheaded brothers, I was able to tell them what I could not tell Nyneve. "I want him to call me son." Saying it, my voice hushed to a whisper.

"No! Mordred, you are insane." Gawain went to his knees—I could not believe it, he knelt before me. "You could be put to death. Do not say it, do not ask it of him. He is the Very King. If he—if he were to call you—what you said—"

"You are his nephew," Garet put in. "Our brother. You cannot be—"

"Hush!" Gawain turned on his brother, then back to me, looking up into my face, pleading. "The land would blacken if he said it. The lakes would boil and turn to poison. The sky would cry blood."

I sat cold, not knowing whether to believe them. Was I, King Arthur's nephew and his son, so very unnatural? If they could think me such a monster, how could they not hate me? Yet Gawain's big, rugged hand lay warm on my knee.

"Mordred, you must not say it, you must not even think it," he begged me. "Never again. Please. Promise."

But—it was my dream he was trying to take from me. "Gawain, I cannot promise you my thoughts!"

"But you will not speak. Mordred, swear it to me."

And I swore. For it was as Gawain said; it would be most unwise for me to call myself the King's son. I could indeed be killed. But even more, I swore for this reason: that always

66

in my dreams it was not I, Mordred, who spoke; it was my father, King Arthur, who acknowledged me. And that was what I truly wanted.

My brothers called for a cot and made me and Gull a bed in a corner of their chamber. In the morning, Gawain would take me to court to look upon my father's face.

6

I COULD NOT SLEEP THAT NIGHT FOR DREAMING OF KING Arthur. I would keep the vow I had sworn to Gawain, to be silent; it would be better that way. My father would look upon me and see himself in my face. He would reach out to me. He would stand, wavering just a little, and step down from his throne and embrace me. My son, he would say. Prince Mordred.

In the morning I dressed in my best clothing: tunic of bleached cambric and tabard of quilted indigo silk, blue cap, blue leggings, boots—and knew it to be not nearly good enough. Gawain and Garet took me to the kitchen, but I could not eat. Gawain jested with the serving folk, but I could not smile. When he had eaten, he led me through a maze of passageways—this castle was as bewildering in its way as the Forest Perilous, this Camelot. Vast and towering and labyrinthine. But not green-shadow dim; even inside,

Camelot shone white. The courtyard, where Gawain led me, glowed with sunlight.

In the sunlight sat a blind harper, an old man in a simple robe of brown homespun, playing on his harp and chanting a ballad:

> . . . *Down in yonder green field*
> *Lies a knight slain under his shield.*
> *His hounds lie down at his feet*
> *To guard him in his final sleep.*
> *His hawks fly a watch so fierce*
> *No carrion bird dares to come near.*
> *Down there comes a fair red doe*
> *Great with fawn, weighted with sorrow.*
> *She kissed him on his bloody head.*
> *She carried him to his earthen bed.*
> *She buried him in day's first light.*
> *She was dead herself by gray twilight.*
> *May the gods give every knight*
> *Such hawks, such hounds, such a lady love . . .*

The wonder of the song rang through me, yet made me cold. Might the gods give me life rather than such a death, I thought, but then I put the thought away from me in shame. A coward's thought.

The blind harper chanted on, his eyes staring as milk white as the towers of Camelot, as white as his beard. On his shoulder there perched a raven, a wise bird with a great black heavy bill that made me think of an executioner's ax. The harper did not see me walking by, of course, but the raven saw me and croaked, "Branded, branded! Red-handed!" Those who had gathered to hear the harper laughed at its cheekiness, but I shivered, for I felt as if it spoke straight to me.

Yet—yet there was no reason for me to feel that way. I was King Arthur's son.

Firming my face, lifting my head, I followed Gawain into the great hall with Gull pattering at my heels.

Even now, after all the years, I remember the great hall of Camelot, that aspiring vaulted hall hung with many tapestries embroidered in threads of red, royal blue, gold. I remember the tapestries: a white stag leaping, a red dragon, a lady in a garden of blue roses, many others. But that morning I saw nothing of their splendor, for my heart pounded like a war stallion charging and I could not think of anything but him, my father. At last.

Blinking in the muted light, I looked for a throne. I saw none.

Yet I knew him at once. King Arthur.

There he sat at his place upon the rim of the Round Table, and by that time he had ruled for more years than I was old. Yet he turned toward me the face of a young man at the height of his powers. No gray dulled the bronze of his beard or his hair curling crisp under his golden crown. He held his chin high as he scanned me with the sea-gray eyes of a visionary. He looked wise, regal, strong, fierce, and fair, an eagle among men, all that a King should be, and what was more to me, he was a man any daydreaming boy would choose as a father.

Such awe and longing washed through me that I could barely stand; weakness as much as courtesy made me fold to my knees at his side. He looked at me quizzically, then up at Gawain, who had not kneeled.

"My brother Mordred, Liege."

King Arthur's face did not change except that his smile widened, his mouth quirking at the corners. He looked straight into my face. "Mordred," he said, "well come."

Surely he felt the irony. What could he have been thinking as he looked upon me, a skinny squire kneeling there, his bastard son fated to kill him? Perhaps he looked for something of himself in me. For my part, I wanted to lay claim to everything that was kingly about him; I searched his face for any sign of me, but saw none.

"Ask of me a boon," he told me, "and I will grant it to you."

How had I dared to think he might call me "son"? His courtesy was marvel enough. "But . . . but Sire," I stammered, "I have not earned—"

"You are Gawain's brother. Is that not worthiness enough? Speak."

Still on my knees, I stared mutely back at him. When I looked upon him, it seemed right and fitting and just that he had tried to kill me when I was a baby; a King cannot be held to blame for any bloody act in defense of his throne. Why did he not kill me now? Why did he not call his guards to take me away and slay me? But there I knelt, within arm's reach of him, and he was offering me a boon because I was Gawain's brother.

I glanced up at Gawain to see him smiling proudly. I noticed the sword scars on his face. "My King," he said, "there is no need for such words."

"There is every need. It is seldom enough that I give you the soft words you deserve." King Arthur turned to me, motioning me to my feet. "Of all my knights, Mordred, your brother Gawain is the one I most greatly trust. If I had to take my soul out of my body and give it to someone for safekeeping, he would be that man."

"My liege!" Gawain protested.

"It is true."

"But you need not say it."

"I am the King, and I will say what I like."

For some reason that started him and Gawain laughing. These jokes and understandings between people left me out in the cold. It seemed as if I was born old and serious. They laughed, and I stood silent, but Gull wagged her tail and barked.

King Arthur peered at her. "Greetings, brachet! Well met." He patted her and rubbed her sides. "You're a fine brachet." His smile turned puzzled. "Is this Nyneve's? But it can't be. That was long ago."

"She's mine, my liege," I said.

"Good, Mordred." Glancing up at me, King Arthur nodded as if I had done something to praise, but what? He straightened in his seat to face me. "Cherish her well. Now ask of me your boon."

He had already given me a boon by touching Gull, but I did not know it. I could not think. The usual thing would have been to ask for a horse and arms, but—was I ready to be a knight? No, many times no, to my shame. I said, "Sire, may I ask the boon of you some other time?"

"Do so."

Thus ended my first audience with King Arthur.

Once again in the white and golden courtyard, I stood dazed, blinking. Gawain thumped me on the shoulder and left me, going off whistling to find his lady. The blind harper was still playing, his back to me; the raven on his shoulder did not see me, for which I was grateful. He strummed the lay of Iseult the Fair, and I listened with my throat aching for the sake of the beauty of the music and the tragedy of the lovers and the glory of Camelot.

Others listened also, among them a few silken-gowned damsels and their maidservants. I saw heads turn my way, as was natural, for I was a stranger, but still, the glances made me shy. I would have gone away except that the music held me.

When the last notes of the song had echoed and faded between the white towers, I sighed, and turned to leave, and there in my path stood a maidservant waiting to speak with me. "My lady mistress sends greetings," she said with a bold, coy look, "and requests to know your name and lineage."

She took me so much by surprise that I could think of no pretty speeches; I merely blurted out what she wanted to know. "Mordred of Lothian."

Her face paled and slackened with horror. She shrank back as if I had put a curse on her, then stumbled away.

It was not always like that. Sometimes folk whispered behind their hands as I passed, but other times, other folk were pleasant to me. Yet when someone gave me a friendly greeting, I always wondered: Was it because they did not know who I was? Did they not see the Mordred mark on me, the X of my destiny hiding under my hair behind my ear? Their courtesy seemed of no account.

All the more remarkable, then, was the courtesy of King Arthur.

Because of him, Arthur, jewel of kings, my early days at Camelot shine bright in my memory. An unproved youth, I squired for Gawain or Garet, riding out with them to go hunting or hawking, carrying notes and tokens to their ladies, looking after their lances and swords, arming them for tournaments and helping them onto their chargers and handing them their shields. And riding with them on adventures, sometimes, into the Forest Perilous. But it is not the tourneys or the adventures that I remember. It is odd things, little things:

Pelleas on a blood-red charger, riding away eastward with the white falcon flying above him, bound on a long quest for a magical cauldron called the Grail.

Nyneve, her chestnut hair and green gown gilded by torchlight, dancing with King Arthur while Guinevere looked on.

A young knight, Sir Torre, greeting me, telling me with greatest good cheer, "I'm Pellinore's bastard." Smiling at me. "There's no shame in being a bastard, Mordred."

King Arthur tripping over Gull and saying to her, "I beg your pardon, brachet."

The blind harper—I happened to look from the topmost tower at sunset, and far to the west I saw a solitary figure on a crag, black against the bright sky. It was the blind harper, who that day had left Camelot, slowly walking toward Cornwall, his raven on his shoulder.

Gawain riding forth in only chain mail, and refusing to yield the road to a haughty French knight in full armor, and sending him over his horse's tail with the lance, then driving him to the ground with the sword, and when the French knight demanded to know who had defeated him, telling him to mortify him, "A humble yeoman of King Arthur's mighty court."

King Arthur in the meadow with the royal horses, great white mares and their mighty black colts, riding the wild colts bareback one after another, laughing, calling to me, "Choose which one you want for yourself, Mordred."

King Arthur remarking to me, "Unless I am much mistaken, Mordred, your brachet is in whelp."

King Arthur riding to tourney on a white destrier as I watched him, thinking what it might mean to be a knight of the Round Table and face lances and swords for his sake.

King Arthur sentencing a deserter to death. The man wept for mercy, but King Arthur gave no mercy. "You have done the deed and you must bear the punishment," he said, and his gray-eyed gaze strayed to me.

"I should go away," I said to Nyneve.

In the top room of her tower, standing at the window, she turned troubled eyes to me.

I said, "When Arthur was my age, he was King, he was

putting down the rebels, he was fighting for his throne and his life." In a year or so I would be knighted, but I did not think I would ever be worthy to serve him.

Nyneve smiled, though the smile did not take away the sadness in her eyes. "You like him."

"Yes. No. I don't know." My first summer in Camelot was over, and I dreaded harvest and winter, the season of gifts. "He is—he is all generosity." King Arthur singled me out for special favor, he gave to me and gave to me, and with each gift he gave me I felt more keenly that he had not gifted me with the words "my son."

And never would, I knew. Damn my foolish longings; in the plain light of day I knew well enough what would happen if King Arthur named me son. It was as Gawain had said, the land would blacken and the lakes would boil. Barons would roar and rebel. Thousands of men would march to war.

Arthur, Very King, was wedded to his realm even more surely than he was wedded to his beloved Guinevere. He would never risk fifteen years of hard-won peace for my sake. He would kill me first.

As he had tried to do already.

I hated him.

No. Damn my childish hatred. I said to Nyneve, "He is all goodness." King Arthur, the rose among kings, golden, fearsome, generous and just—I adored him. "I mean it; I should leave. No good can come of my being here."

"Has not good come of it already? In you? In what you feel for him?"

I shrugged, angry at myself because my voice had betrayed emotion. "Let us go down to the courtyard." And speak of other things. "Come, Nyneve, you will turn into an owl up here." She spent too much time in her tower, gazing from her window, eastward, the way Pelleas had gone.

She made a face at me and quipped, "I should go away."

Her mockery was gentle, as always. I rolled my eyes and offered her my arm. "Come, let us stroll in the sunshine."

In the courtyard we found many folk enjoying the last of the good weather—little children and their nurses, stable-boys, soldiers, lords in tunics of indigo velvet, ladies in satin gowns. Gawain was there with the maiden he was courting at the moment, offering her a bouquet of asters—he looked only to her, but many others looked to me, silent, wary. They moved away from me, then turned to stare. It was always thus when I went among castle folk. Camelot had heard the prophecy. Camelot was watching.

Instead of answering their stares, I looked at Nyneve, at her flower of a face, fair and pale—too pale. She was often pale these days. Only leather bound her braids, no gold, and she wore no gold on her gown, not even a brooch. I wished I could give her an aster to put in her hair.

"He will come back to you," I told her.

She darted a glance at me, startled, then smiled—but it was not her merry smile. "The mirror is muddy," she said. "I cannot see."

"But you would know if he were—" I did not wish to say it.

"I am not sure. The Grail is a fearsome thing." She turned

away from me, looking toward the gates, then up at the soaring white walls as if she wanted to fly out of that place. "His quest takes him farther from me than I know how to say."

Pelleas was a friend to me before he left. Most folk would give me only a stare; Pelleas would give me a smile and a greeting, but a glare and no greeting to Gawain, upon whom most folk smiled. I meant sometime to ask Nyneve why. Not now.

I grew weary of feeling folk's stares. I asked Nyneve, "Shall we walk out on the meadows?"

"Yes."

We turned toward the gates. But just then there sounded a clattering, and a heavy ringing of hooves on cobbles, and cries as folk scrambled out of the way. In rode a massive, harsh-bearded knight in battered armor.

"Pellinore," Nyneve whispered, stepping back.

Nyneve was not the only damsel who feared him. I had heard by then how Sir Pellinore had begotten Torre upon a milkmaid. Rode up and seized her and raped her and rode away again.

Pellinore sent his charger into the courtyard at a ramping trot as if he did not care whether he might trample someone. Even lords and ladies had to get out of his way as he rode through with his armor clashing—he wore full, heavy armor and a broadsword as long as my arm. Froth foamed from his charger's mouth, splattering the silks of the ladies he passed. A stench issued off him. His shield was hacked, his armor ravaged with sword cuts and spotted with rust from months in the field, and—I gasped. Slung from his saddle, tied there by its hair, hung a human head.

I looked again, for I was seeing what it truly meant to be a knight, a fighter—and then I felt my knees weaken. I had to clutch Nyneve's shoulder to steady myself. That head—it seemed to look back at me with its sunken eyes, to curse me with its decaying mouth. I knew it. Even though it hung dead from Pellinore's saddle, I knew it: the head of King Lothe.

7

SOME PEOPLE FIND BLOOD PRETTY, THE BRIGHTEST OF BRIGHT reds, brighter than the poppy flower, brighter than the pimpernel. I find blood ugly.

Blood colored the rest of that year in Camelot for me.

From the moment that Pellinore rode in with King Lothe's head at his knee, it was plain to Gawain and Garet that Pellinore had to be killed. It was equally plain to them that I would help them. And as Pellinore was a knight of the Round Table, he could not be challenged; he would have to be ambushed.

"But that's three against one," I said.

"What do I care?" In our chamber, Gawain sat drinking his sixth or seventh mug of hard mead; he glared at me, half weeping, half savage. He had seen King Lothe's head. Garet had not seen it; Garet sat more sober.

"But—if this Pellinore killed your father as he says he did, in fair combat—"

Only the table and his own drunkenness kept Gawain from lunging at me. "Fair?" His flushed face jutted toward mine like a gargoyle. "Fair fight, to wear our father's head as a trophy?" It had fallen to me to go to Pellinore and see if I could get Lothe's head back, for burial, but he had already fed it to the kennel dogs, he said. A paragon of chivalry, Pellinore. "I plan to haul him from the horse and tie him to a tree—"

I did not want to hear this. "But that's *murder.*"

"Murder?" Gawain surprised me; he leaned back and began to laugh. "Why, we'll all be murderers together, then. Show me someone in this world who is not a murderer. I'm a murderer, our mother, Morgause, is a murderer, our aunt Morgan is a murderer, our uncle King Arthur—"

"Gawain!" Garet protested.

"You're drunk," I said.

"You don't believe me? What else do you call it when he kills thirty-nine others trying to kill you?"

"Gawain!" Garet stood to hush him. I, also, got up, not knowing where I was going. I stood there, my heart stuttering like my mouth. "Wh-wh-what?"

"Babies," Gawain snarled. I could not tell what he was saying, whether our mother, Morgause, had killed babies—which she might have, I had sometimes wondered, our baby sisters all dead—or whether he was calling Garet and me babies, or—I was not sure he had said what I thought I had heard; he had said something of King Arthur—

"Gawain," Garet warned, "speak no more, not a single word."

Gawain did not obey, of course. "And your precious Nyneve," he barked at me, blurring the words, "she's a murderer too."

He was drunk. Not worth answering. I turned my back on him and walked out of our chamber.

I went looking for Nyneve and found her, not in her tower, but by the central fountain in Queen Guinevere's garden— the one place in Camelot where Gull was not allowed to follow me. It was a peaceful place, that garden, full of order and symmetry, quite unlike the twisted wilderness outside the castle walls. A high square of hedge enclosed it for shade and silence, and inside, straight white-cobbled paths ran under trellises of roses—any churl can grow violets, but a noble garden fosters great roses, red and white, and beds of lilies and carnations. Fruit trees stood in the garden too, apple, pear, pomegranate, their fruit hanging as yellow and red and heavy as the flowers. And in the trees, golden cages held linnets and blackbirds and nightingales. I felt bad for the birds—would not sweetly singing birds have winged to those trees without being caged there? Still, it was a royal garden, a jewel among gardens, heady with roses, a fitting haven for the Queen. Few folk were allowed there, but Nyneve was a favored courtier, and so was I. King Arthur cosseted me, and so, perforce, did the Queen.

On the soft turf by the fountain, Nyneve sat gazing into the water even though it stirred constantly and she could see nothing there. After encountering Pellinore, she had made her way to water for comfort, I knew, just as I had made my way to her.

When my shadow fell on her, she looked up at me with a

small smile. I sat beside her and watched the fountain water sprinkling down. In the basin swam rose petals—white, yellow, pink, red—and under the petals, small golden fish. There was no darkness in the water. "Not ladywater," I remarked.

"No. This is shallow water."

We sat in silence, and I felt the hardness of my shoulders begin to ease, and I sighed.

Nyneve asked, "How is Gawain?"

"Drinking himself into a rage."

"And Garet?"

"Not much better."

She nodded, knowing much without my telling her. "It will be nasty. These things can go on for years. Sir Torre is Pellinore's son. Sir Lamorak, Sir Percival, Sir Agrivale, Sir Dornar, they're all his sons. They will all be honor bound to avenge him if Gawain harms him."

There was so much troubling me that I could speak only around the edges of it. I said, "Gawain claims we are all murderers."

"Did he speak for himself?"

"Yes. How—"

"His first quest. He defeated a strong knight. The man lay on the ground begging for mercy, but Gawain swung his sword to kill him. As the blow fell, the knight's lady threw herself in the way, and Gawain could not stop the sword. He beheaded her."

I sat dumbfounded. My brother Gawain, whom everyone adored, had done this evil thing?

But why not? The world was crazy. I, whom everyone

loathed, I had done nothing, but King Arthur, whom everyone adored—King Arthur had tried to kill—

I shook my head, shaking the thoughts away. I said, "Pelleas acts as if he hates Gawain. Is that why?"

"No."

A curt reply. Whatever lay wrong between Pelleas and Gawain, Nyneve did not wish to speak of it. Or perhaps she did not wish to be reminded of Pelleas. Perhaps she wished I would go away and let her alone. But I could not.

"Gawain says that you, also, are a murderer."

"Some folk might see it that way." She turned to me, her calm eyes dark with the suffering that had been in them since Pelleas rode away. "After that brute Sir Outelake, the next knight who seized me, I waited until he took off his mail and then I put my dagger in him. Then I cut off his head with his own sword. And then I rode his charger instead of my little palfrey, and yes, I hung his head at my knee until it stank. After that, the ruffians let me alone." She watched me, her gaze like deep water, hiding her thoughts. "Was it murder, do you think?"

"I—I don't know." Most folk would not think a knight deserved to die just for trying to ravish a pretty maiden.

"I would not need to kill him now," Nyneve said. "I would fell him with a touch of my hands. But I did not learn that power until Merlin taught me." She turned back to staring at the water. "And he taught me only because he wanted something in return. He wanted me in just the same way as the others."

But why had he not used his magic to overpower her, then? "Was he—was he not fated to love you?"

"Fate is a lie, Mordred." Her stare turned as fierce as a falcon's glare, fit to harden the water. "Fate is Merlin's puffery. He was saving his pride. He knew I might best him; if he said it was his fate, then he could appear to go nobly to his doom. And if he escaped, he would seem all the more mighty." Her glare softened. "As it turned out, I bested him."

She had shut him in a cave in Cornwall, some of the tales said, with a great stone closing the entrance for all eternity. She had laid him alive in his tomb, others said. She had imprisoned him in a hill of glass, said yet others, or in the trunk of a great tree. I did not ask her which of the tales was true. I did not want to know.

I gazed upon her, seeing with my heart how the sunlight rippled on her russet hair, remembering that the bards said that Merlin had followed her like a dog. The sun warmed my shoulders, yet I shivered in the shadow of her power.

"Can you see the future?" I asked abruptly.

"No."

"If you had ladywater to scry in?"

"No. I cannot prophesy. That is the one power Merlin could not teach me."

Though I did not like to think that she would lie to me, I did not entirely believe her. Or, if I believed her, was she saying then that Merlin had been a true prophet?

And if Merlin was a prophet, then—then it would be as Merlin had said, I would—kill—

"I am heartsick, Mordred," Nyneve said softly, looking at the water, not at me, as she spoke. "I am going home. Perhaps not even my Lady can comfort me, but I am going home to Avalon."

I said nothing, knowing that I would be like a pennon blowing in the wind without her.

Yet—yet it might be better if I depended less on her advice. Folk looked down on a man who listened too much to a woman.

"Journey well," I said finally, speaking just as softly as she did.

"Yes." She rose from the grass. "Thank you, Mordred."

I struggled up, my sense of doom riding heavy in me. "Before you go—can you truly not see my path, Nyneve? Can you not tell me what is to become of me?"

She gave me a look as hard and straight as a sword. "It is up to you, Mordred, what will become of you."

"Have a whack at him, Mordred!" Gawain cried.

He and Garet had done just as they had said they would. They had overpowered Pellinore, stripped him of his armor, slapped his face to shame him, and tied him to an oak in the Forest Perilous as I, their squire, held the horses. Now they were killing him in painful ways. And Gawain was offering me a turn.

"Go ahead!" He thrust at me the pommel of his bloodied sword.

I shook my head. I could not look at him.

"What," Garet put in, "you don't like this game?"

Gawain complained, "Be a man, Mordred!"

That lout Pellinore was a man, I will give him that. He had not begged, he would not speak except to curse, and he had not yet cried out. Tied to the tree, bleeding, he stood with his head up, glaring like a wild boar.

"Last chance!" Gawain persisted in wanting to share with me his bloody deed, offering me the sword, his gloved hand stained dark and wet.

"No," I whispered. I said it again somewhat more strongly. "No. Your father was not my father."

At the tree, Pellinore barked out a harsh laugh. Gawain whirled and struck him hard across the face with the flat of the blade. "Coward," Garet accused me.

True enough. If I were not such a coward, I would not have come with them at all.

"How do you ever expect to be a knight?" grumbled Gawain, disgusted with me.

They turned their backs on me and—and they went on with it. I wish to say no more. Standing back, clutching three pairs of reins, I lowered my eyes and would not watch—but I could not close my ears. I heard my brothers jeering. I heard their blades thudding into flesh. I heard the screams—toward the end, Pellinore could not help but scream.

When he fell silent, I looked up. That was a mistake. I had not known there was so much blood in a man.

Later, back in our chamber in Camelot, I cleaned the weapons. That was my job. Then I gathered my things and bundled them. Sitting and drinking, my brothers did not notice at first.

"Mordred, what are you doing?" Gawain exclaimed as I hefted my belongings and headed out the door.

"You don't have to go. You can't help it that you're a coward," Garet told me quite sincerely.

"There's too much I can't help," I told him.

I moved into Nyneve's empty tower. Folk talked, of

course, and wanted to know why, and I am sure Gawain and Garet gave them an explanation. Thus began my reputation for cowardice.

Thus began also my time of being alone. I had no lady; most damsels seemed afraid of me. Nyneve, my friend and mentor, was gone. I still served Gawain and Garet as their squire, but we were silent, shame had come between us, and they called on me less often.

I thought sometimes: What was the Round Table, truly, that it honored knights such as Sir Pellinore? And Sir Gawain?

I went seldom to court. The place in Camelot where I felt most at peace those winter days was the kennel, lying in a warm nest of straw with Gull and her pups.

Yes, pups. It was as King Arthur had said: Gull had whelped a litter at last, seven handsome round little brachets and brach-hounds as blind and soft as so many moles, three of them white, three spotted, and one as black as night. Gull had given birth to them in my bedchamber in Nyneve's tower, but Kay, the seneschal, had suggested to me in decided tones that the kennel was a more fitting place for puppies, so to the kennel they went, and of course Gull had to stay there with them. And I spent hours every day there with Gull. At one time or another I had my face licked by every dog in the kennel, from the great fierce-toothed mastiffs and willowy gazehounds to the tiny terriers; maidens did not care for me, but dogs adored me.

In the kennel, I would let Gull's puppies crawl upon me and nuzzle my throat with their blunt heads as I lay in the straw and tried to sense what I should do. I should leave, I had said to Nyneve. I should leave, I had said also to Gawain more recently. "You just hold up your head," he said. "No brother of mine is a coward." But I was a coward, and therefore not his brother, so why did I stay?

"Mordred."

I blinked and looked up. Standing as he was in the brightness of the doorway, and lying as I was in the shadows, I saw at first only a tall form haloed in golden glory, as if he were an angel.

"My liege?" I lifted three of the puppies away from me and started to scramble up.

"No, stay." King Arthur came in and sat on a bale of straw close by. "You're wise. It's warm in here." Flushed from cold, he threw back his deep-dyed blue mantle, then spoke gravely to Gull, who was lying flat on her side in the straw, thumping her tail at him, as the other four puppies suckled. "Greetings, brachet. You're a good brachet to make such fine pups."

Just the month before, I had seen the folk lined up at Camelot's gate by the hundred on the first day of the new moon: sickly children, old people with goiters or gout or scrofula, cripples, folk from all over the realm in need of the King's touch. I understood that part of being a Very King was to be a healer.

"The brachet thanks you for taking away her barrenness," I said, trying to match King Arthur's whimsical tone, wondering why he could not take away the barrenness of Queen Guinevere.

He gave me a wry half smile. "She's welcome."

We sat in silence as I tried to think why he might be there and as my heart struggled with the clashing emotions I always felt in his presence, the yearning and resentment.

No. I lie. I do not like to say truly what my feelings were: love and hatred. I did not care to use those words then—but how I loved him, my great-hearted King, because he smiled on me, and how I hated him because he would do anything for me, anything, except embrace me as his son.

"I am sorry about this ugliness with Pellinore, Mordred," he said, looking not at me but at Gull. "First you lose your father—"

"He was not my father." Sudden anger jolted my spine as straight as a lance, and the words were out, hard and strong, before I could fear them. Hard and level I was glaring into my liege King Arthur's eyes.

Then my heart stopped. I stopped breathing. He had to know what I was thinking. Would he call the guards and have them take me away, or would he—would he say it?

Neither. He met my stare for a hollow moment, and then his gray gaze shifted. He looked down, he almost seemed to redden. My heart started beating again, and aching, for I wanted never to see King Arthur ashamed.

"Your foster father, I mean," he said quietly. "King Lothe. I am sorry."

"King Lothe meant nothing to me but a beating from time to time." How could I be so calm, so cold?

In the straw Gull sprawled, snoring, soft bellied, one ear flopped the wrong direction and turned inside out so that its pink innards showed. King Arthur and I sat and studied her as if we had never seen a brachet before.

"But I, also, am sorry," I said, my voice low. I was not speaking of King Lothe.

"Yes. Well, this trouble . . ." King Arthur stirred almost painfully on his throne of straw. "I have told your brothers that a man of courage and sense chooses his own fight. I have also told them that it is time we provided you with horse and arms." He gave me a level look. "Will you serve me, Mordred, as a knight of the Round Table?"

"But . . . but my liege!" Now I was the one astonished and hot with shame. I stammered, "You . . . you would knight me? I will be greatly honored, but . . . I have done nothing to make me worthy."

He did not smile at my emotion. I will cherish him always because he did not smile. He said, "Sometimes worthiness comes afterward."

"I . . . I hope so."

King Arthur said quietly, "And sometimes it does not. Remember, Pellinore was a knight of mine."

It was a quelling thought—yet it comforted me that he said it, that we could speak of it. It had troubled me, sometimes, to think that Pellinore had been a Knight of the Round Table.

"Is that why you took him to you, then?" I asked. "In hopes that he might become worthy?"

"Partly, yes. Partly, it was for expediency. I needed to have him and his sons for me, not against me." King Arthur's gaze turned bleak, and looking up at him, I thought of what

I should have asked Nyneve before she left: the meaning of the white stag leaping for life in the Forest Perilous, the black hounds always at its heels.

King Arthur said softly, "Mordred, there's small freedom in being a King. Most often a King does not what he wishes, but what he must."

Often in the days that followed I wondered: Did King Arthur wish to make me his knight? Or was he merely doing what he must?

Thoughts like those sliced like sword cuts. For hours every day I wore myself out smiting foes made of straw in the exercise yard, but I still could not sleep at night.

Worthiness . . .

I had none. All I had was my adoration and my shameful, hidden hatred. That black hatred—I began to know why it stayed with me; it was my fate at work. In me. And I could tell myself and tell myself that a prophecy was a lie, as Nyneve had said, a bogey made of nothing but words, an echo in the wind—yet my body knew the power of prophecy. I could feel the fate pulsing dark in my blood as I tried to sleep; I could feel it lying heavy in my stomach as I tried to eat; I could feel it in me like a black marrow in my bones.

How could I serve King Arthur as his knight? I wanted to go away, I wanted to do what was right, yet I stayed as if skewered on the sword of his goodliness.

Those nights for the first time I thought of killing myself, and the thought frightened me so badly that I walked through my days trembling.

Or perhaps I shook from lack of sleep. Or perhaps because I had not been eating. The world began to look bright and strange to me. Without meaning to, I became like a young druid undergoing a vigil, waiting for a vision.

It came to me as I lay in my bed on the last night before the ceremony of knighthood.

I lay stark awake—it was no mere dream, but a vision. The memory shines like a great jewel, brighter than most waking days of my life. I saw Pelleas riding in a strange country, under a yellow sky, but I did not see the white falcon with him. He rode a white mule, and he rode wearily, and the mule's head hung. He rode into such a garden as I have never seen. The trees wept like fountains, and great birds with trailing tails flew over, making strange cries. In the middle of the garden stood a pleasure pavilion with a roof tiled in gold; Pelleas rode there. And on a bed in the pavilion, Gawain lay sleeping with a maiden in his arms. Pelleas looked for a long moment at Gawain and the maiden, but he did not awaken them. He laid his naked sword across their necks, then turned away.

But everything changed. The pleasure pavilion turned to gray stone tower with four doors; at each door stood a gilded woman. The yellow sky turned indigo; it was night. Pelleas's mule became a great white stag with antlers that formed a golden crown. And where Gawain and the lady had lain, there stood a silver cauldron brimming with some liquid that glimmered darkly, like ladywater.

I drew nearer, gazing at the silver cauldron, and saw that it was filled with blood.

Yet in the vision I was not afraid. This blood was not ugly, but beautiful. I gazed as if scrying in a liquid ruby. And in the pool of blood I saw a simple vision, yet a great mystery, as if a serpent nested with a dove. It made me tremble, for it was a seeing not of this world. I saw King Arthur embracing me as a son.

And in that moment I knew what I must do. I knew what my worthiness must be.

And my quest.

And my grail.

BOOK THREE
The White Falcon

8

I RODE AWAY FROM CAMELOT IN THE EARLIEST SPRING, WITH no companion but Gull.

I said nothing to anyone until the days grew warm enough for me to leave, and then only to King Arthur. I was lucky to find him alone, sitting in his chamber, a leather-bound Plutarch on his knee—it was more study than bedchamber, his room, vellum charts pegged to the walls, a cot no wider or softer than mine. There I was able to speak to him privately, formally, bowing on one knee before him.

"Arise, Sir Mordred." It was an echo of the night of my dubbing, when the Round Table watched and King Arthur lifted the sword from my shoulder and called me for the first time by my knightly name.

I rose. "I beg leave to pursue a quest, Sire."

"A quest, Sir Mordred? What quest?"

Keeping my voice very low, I said, "A quest to save us both, my King."

To save his life.

And my soul.

He drew one quick breath, almost a gasp. I think I saw his eyes glimmer, wet. His lips parted, but then he pressed them shut again, as if he did not dare to ask what I meant. He knew.

"Go with my blessing." He stood, lifting his hands as if he would place them on my head, although he did not touch me. I think he had never touched me except with the sword when he knighted me. "Take a spare horse with you. And take a pack mule, and supplies. And choose yourself a squire."

But I rode forth from the gates of Camelot alone except for Gull, and no one waved me on my way.

"You're not worried about your puppies, Gull," I asked her, "are you?" They were old enough to get along without her.

She gave me a gentle look that might or might not have been an answer, then trotted in front of me, her tail uplifted like my lance. King Arthur had gifted me with the lance and a fine sword of Damascene steel and all my arms and gear. I carried, slung around my neck until I might need it, the blank white shield of a new and unblooded knight. I wore good chain mail and a light helm with a nosepiece, a light breastplate, and greaves on my legs, but other than that no body armor—I knew I was not strong enough to carry such weight. Someday I might be, perhaps, but I was not yet sixteen years old; I was as tall as most men in Camelot, but slender. If I fought, I would have to be faster than my opponent or quicker of wit. But I knew that I would not find what I was seeking by fighting.

Or, at least, not by fighting ordinary foes.

"Gull," I called to her, "we're going south. Toward the sea." This time I would lead, not she.

It was likely to be a long road into eerie places. But I would find my way. I would find a way out of the doom Merlin had laid on me. I would fight my fate.

To love the sea, I knew, was to love my enemy. When I was a baby, the sea had taken me away from my kinfolk and my mother, starved me, sprayed salt on my tender naked skin, tried to freeze me in its chill embrace, tried to kill me. To love the sea was to love what I ought to hate.

This showed at least that it was possible. For I did love the sea.

I rode southward on a cart trail that led through the fringes of the Forest Perilous, and my heart beat faster at the thought of looking out again over vast water, breathing sea-scented air, hearing once again the cries of the gulls. But I had not ridden an hour before I encountered my first challenger.

I was to grow accustomed to meeting with knights-errant three or four times a day. The rule of King Arthur's reign was that knights were to fight each other and leave the common folk alone. Camelot was, as I have said, a castle under a spell; the whole realm was rife with knights blundering about, trying to find it, and they all seemed to be in foul temper.

Like this one. In full armor, he burst out of a rowan grove with his lance leveled, charging at me. "Sir, if you love your honor, prepare to joust!" he roared.

In that moment I decided that I loved other things, including my life, far more than my honor. He was taller than I, weighed probably eight stone more, he wore a great heavy sword fit to fell a tree with, and he had not given me time even to buckle on my shield. I couched my lance and met him, but I aimed at his horse's head. Before his lance could reach me, his poor blameless mount fell down dead. He rolled free of the body and struggled to his feet, drawing his sword, bellowing with rage. "Get down from your horse, coward, and fight!"

"Thank you for the kind offer," I told him, "but I think not." I turned my back on him and rode away.

I was to grow accustomed to being called a coward. Three or four times a day.

That first day, however, I met no knights after noon. Blessedly, I left the Forest Perilous behind and challengers with it. I crossed a salty grassland, and—there was the sea. There were the rocks and the gravel shore and the gray glinting water stretching to eternity and oh, but I was glad to stand under wide sky again. In a sheltered cove, a kind of natural harbor, stood a quay, by which a coracle rocked like a cradle on the waves. Far overhead soared an erne, the eagle of the sea.

For three days I traveled along the sea, eating mussels and curlew eggs, falling asleep to the murmur of the waves, scarcely admitting even to myself whom I was seeking: a little boy named Tad, he who was the gift of Lyr, he who was happy.

On the third day, I thought I found him.

I rounded a point of rock and felt the pang in my heart before my mind began to comprehend. I looked down a stretch of shore like all others, gravel and sandpipers and rugged brown rock, yet my heart yearned like the crying of a gull; in my chest Tad awoke and knew these rocks as surely as if they were Fishermother's coarse, kindly brown face.

A few more strides of my steed, and I saw the hut, and then I understood.

Seemingly all by itself, my mouth gave forth a soft cry like a sigh. I rode forward slowly, staring.

"Gull," I whispered, for my heart was beating so hard I had to speak to someone, "this is my home."

But no one came to the door. No round brown face looked out at me. I began to grow afraid.

I halted where I was. I got down from my horse and let it graze on the coarse salt grass as I sat on the rocks, looking down on the fisherhut with the soundless ringing of bluebells in my ears.

I sat there with Gull beside me, my mail catching the sun and cooking me, until day dimmed into evening. In the slanting orange light I saw Fisherfather's coracle bobbing in to land, dark on the bright water. I saw him heave himself out of the boat and wade to shore. I saw a lad get out and help him drag the boat up on the beach for the night.

Then Fisherfather stopped what he was doing as he caught sight of me sitting there on the rocks. They both stared. I got up, stiff from sitting, and walked down to them with Gull trotting beside me.

"My lord?" Fisherfather looked old and tired and frightened. He and the young churl both stood bobbing their heads and pulling their forelocks, uncertain whether they must kneel, their faces so much alike that I knew the boy must be his son—the baby Nyneve had felt in Fishermother.

"No need to call me lord," I told him. "You used to call me Tad."

He gawked at me anew.

I said quietly, "She's dead, isn't she?"

"Pardon, my—" He caught himself before he said "lord."

"Your wife."

"Ay, she's dead. She died in the birthing of Kip here."

The boy stood watching me, tired, like his father, and sullen also. Likely he envied me my great black charger and my shiny mail and my shiny white shield and my sword of Damascene steel, but I smelled the salt and heard the wash of the waves close to my feet and saw the terns flying to land for the night, and I would have traded places with him in a moment.

"She's been dead these nine years," Fisherfather said in that dank, weary way of his.

I stood watching the terns, their sharp white wings gilded in the late-day light. The fisherman and his son stood watching me.

I was still a lord to them, I realized. They could not move to go about their work until I allowed it. So I said, "Is the catch good?" and that let them haul it out of the boat to show me.

Yes, it was a good catch. We had fish chowder for supper. I stayed with them that night, sleeping on their dirt floor near their warm hearth, and I stayed the next day, riding along with them as they took their salted herring to market, and they grew easier with me. They did not call me Tad, of course, they could not, but neither did they call me Mordred. Nor did they my-lord me. They called me nothing. It felt good to be nothing. I stayed the next day as well.

That night, late, after Kip was asleep, Fisherfather settled himself on his three-legged stool by the hut's frugal fire and began to speak of Fishermother. "If we had not meddled in the affairs of nobles," he said, "Bess would still be alive."

Bess. So that was her name. I had never known it.

"That sorceress friend of yours put a curse on her, so she did." Fisherfather said this with a sodden, crusty anger that bore me no grudge. They learn to accept all things, these common folk.

I could not think that Nyneve would have done such a thing. Yet I had heard myself the ringing of the bluebells. Did they doom her? Or did they merely foretell?

Night wrapped around the hut like a black wool blanket, like Fishermother's arms. A quiet night—I heard only the sounds of soft breathing: Gull, Kip, the broad sleeping breast of the sea. The silence of the night by the warm dim hearth fire made me able to ask a question I could not even think before.

"When you found me," I said, "when you found the coracle—were there other babies in it?"

Silence. A long moment of silence before he answered as quietly as I had asked.

"Ay. Many. All dead but you."

Silence again. My fisherfather leaned forward and with a crooked stick he stirred the fire, sending up a flicker of light.

"The wee bodies lay in the boat like so many pollack," he said. "I'll never forget. Many was the night I lost my sleep for thinking of it."

I sat thinking bitterly of the stories my fishermother had told me. I, Tad, the gift of Lyr, her miracle.

"Bess didn't know about the others," my fisherfather said. "I didn't tell her. It would have broken her heart entirely."

I began to understand. "You pushed that coracle back into the sea yourself."

"Ay."

Thanks to his kindness, my fishermother had believed her stories, it seemed. But her believing seemed not to make them any less lies. Gift of Lyr? No. She loved me because—because she did not know who I was. I, Mordred. King Arthur's accursed son.

Good King Arthur. Flower of kings, jewel of kings, prince of kings—and murderer. A murderer of babies.

I had looked into his face trying to see something of myself there. I had longed to be more like him.

I, Mordred, fated to be his murderer. Perhaps I resembled him after all.

I had discovered why knights seldom rode so near to the sea: The damp air rusts armor within a few days. I was forever cleaning mine, trying to keep it shining new, the way King Arthur had given it to me.

That night in the fisherman's hut, when the fire dwindled to embers, my fisherfather walked out to check his boat and the height of the tide, and I stayed by the hearth, polishing my helm. As I rubbed the gleaming steel I could not stop thinking of King Arthur—shining King, murderer of babies—and my heart was aching, aching, and the embers pulsed like glowing hearts, giving forth a dim light nearly as red as blood. I set my helm on the floor by the fire and on my knees I rubbed it fiercely. Then I lifted my hand away and looked. I had polished it so well that from the darkly red-shining surface a face looked back at me—

A face not my own.

I gasped, but I'd had enough experience of scrying by then that I did not blink or move. As if the surface of the metal might ripple with a breath, I held still, staring.

It was the face of my aunt. Morgan le Fay.

She wore the rich colors of royalty—crimson, Indy blue, edgings of gold. Something rich hung down behind her, a bed curtain or tapestry. She seemed artfully bestowed, as if she had been waiting for me. She smiled at me, a saucy smile on that white-powdered, apple-cheeked face of hers, and she lifted her hand, plump, white, cuffed with a long ruffle of lace, and beckoned to me: Come hither.

"Why?" I whispered.

She smiled more widely, coy, and beckoned again.

Then the door scraped open and Fisherfather entered, yawning, shuffling with weariness in his clumsy boots. I took the helm and hid it in a saddlebag. Morgan le Fay might smile at leather and canvas if she chose.

9

GULL," I TOLD HER AS I RODE AWAY IN THE MORNING, "I have to do it."

She frisked ahead of me, ears flapping, tail jaunty, as if it did not even matter that I was being summoned by Morgan le Fay. That I was venturing to the stronghold of a sorceress.

"She knows more of uncanny things than anyone, I think. Maybe even more than Nyneve."

Gull halted with her nose seemingly glued to earth, sniffing for a mouse or something, paying no attention to me.

"I wonder what she wants with me," I muttered. Going to see Morgan le Fay was reckless. Going to see her when I knew she wanted me for some purpose of her own was more than reckless; it was mad. "And they call me a coward," I grumbled.

With Gull scampering after me, I rode into the Forest Perilous and was not afraid. I was too terrified of Morgan le Fay to be afraid of a mere lair of thieves, trolls, renegade knights, witches, nixies, seven-headed beasts, and wandering spirits of the dead.

During the next few weeks I encountered stranger things than those.

A slain knight lay in a glade with a maiden weeping over him. "Avenge my brother!" she cried to me. I said to her, "If I were to be killed, no one would avenge me." With rainy eyes she gazed at me in pity, almost in understanding, and I knew I had never seen anyone so beautiful.

I rode past the mouth of a cave, and from the darkness within it something roared. I looked, and eight feet above the ground I saw yellow eyes blazing and a puff of purple fire. I said, "Greetings, denizen," and rode on.

A tall knight on a huge horse barred my path and challenged me, "Sir, defend yourself." He wore a full helm with a visor, and full armor; even his charger wore armor. He couched his lance, but I said, "A lance is an awkward thing to carry in the woodland," and I threw mine into the bracken. He said, "Sir, you are a coward." I said, "Sir, I am not a lunatic," and I rode away.

In the night I heard a sound that resembled the baying of hounds, but when I pulled a flaming stick from my campfire and held it high to look, I saw a beast with a body like that of a leopard but legs and cloven feet like those of a red deer. It turned its head and hissed at me, and its head was that of a great serpent, with flat fiery eyes. I threw my torch at it, and it sprang away.

Two greyhounds leaped out of a thicket and attacked Gull. Snarling, she crouched under my horse, and I smacked the greyhounds with the flat of my sword, trying to drive them away. "How dare you smite my dogs!" a knight bellowed, charging. We fought with swords on horseback, and his heavy weapon sliced me on the arm, the head, the shoulder, then glanced off my shield and severed my horse's neck; the steed fell to the ground, thrashing, and I fell with it. Without dismounting, the knight bore down on me, and I knew I would die, and I saw Gull and the greyhounds watching, all sitting in a row, best friends now—but another knight came galloping with couched lance, and he swept the attacker over the tail of his horse and leaped down and dragged off his helm and beheaded him. "Take this scoundrel's horse," he told me. "Now you're a blooded knight, Sir Mordred," and he rode away; he was Sir Lancelot.

Every night I heard the wolves wailing.

At the rising of the moon I saw, riding across the sky upon a fiery horse, a giant furred man with the antlers of a great stag growing out of his forehead.

I rode past a beech tree and *thwock*, some outlaw's arrow stood in it, buried almost to the feathers, buzzing.

At the roots of the greatest ash tree I had ever seen, so tall its leaves disappeared in cloud, sat an ancient crone, a comely maiden, and a slip of a girl, each with her hair in a thousand tiny plaits beneath a crown of ivy. As I rode toward them, the crone gave me a snaggletoothed smile. "Greetings, Mordred." She spun thread, and as it passed from her crooked hands, it turned many colors. "We're weaving your life now," the maiden told me eagerly, and on her deft hands the thread turned to a mighty jewel-bright complication, a cat's cradle fit to be a dragon's nest. "Time to cut it!" the little girl cried, and she lifted a pair of shears as heavy and black as a raven's beak. "No," said the maiden, "just for fun, let him do it. Mordred, come, you can use your sword." She was just a gentle maiden, but I had never felt so frightened of anyone or anything, not even the serpent-headed beast, not even the horned rider in the sky, not even the arrow out of nowhere meant to kill me. I turned my horse and galloped away.

When at last I arrived at Caer Morgana, the stronghold of my aunt Morgan le Fay, I was able to present her with a gift of two fine greyhounds.

"My nephew Mordred!" she cried when the servants showed me to her solarium, mocking her own lack of surprise to see me as I bowed before her, shabby and weary, my wounds half healed. She smiled like a cat, perhaps thinking that I was doubly her nephew. "And what are these?" The graceful gazehounds had come in with me.

"For you, my lady."

"A perfect brace! My thanks. Take them to the kennel," she told the servants, "and this brachet with them."

"No," I said, "Gull stays with me."

She rolled her eyes, but permitted it. She wished to befriend me, then, at least at the start. Good. The servants showed me to a lofty chamber with cages of linnets and partridges hanging from the vaulted ceiling, with mullioned windows glassed in many colors as bright as flowers. They

brought me a warm, petal-strewn bath and new clothing—
a fine white cambric undertunic, a red velvet tunic, a tabard
of golden damask. When I was robed, a maidservant
brought perfumed balm for my wounds. By the time I went
down for dinner I felt almost safe in Caer Morgana.

It was a place less a stronghold than a pleasure palace.
The courtyards spread wide, and the halls also, not stony
and cramped like the halls of Lothian or even Camelot.
Many windows let in the light. From my tower chamber I
could see a river rushing in a deep ravine, and this seemed to
be all that set apart Caer Morgana from the Forest Perilous;
I saw no moat. Morgan le Fay had her own ways of defending herself and her lands, as I came to understand.

We dined in her bedchamber, instead of in the common
room. Servants had placed a table between the windows,
and brought in wine and sweet breads for just the two of us.

"Is this the way to dine," I tried to joke, "when you are a
great lady with no husband?"

She smiled. "Is it not more pleasant here than in a smoky,
drafty hall?"

Indeed it was, with the tapestries hanging lush around us
and scented rushes lying deep on the floor and beeswax candles for light. And the lady—in the candle glow I could almost forget she was my aunt Morgan le Fay and think of her
just as a lady—the lady was pleasant to look at, gowned in
the Byzantine fashion, draped in scarves, with her hair lifted
by gold wire into a complication as dense as that dragon's
nest I had seen in the Forest Perilous.

"Aside from that," Morgan added, "I would like to be

able to speak frankly to you, with no one listening from the shadows."

I remembered how I had eavesdropped as a child in Lothian and smiled. "Of what shall we speak so frankly?" I asked, for I wished to know what was her game, as King Lothe would have put it.

"Why, gossip, of course. Did you know that your mother has taken a lover?"

I did not, and the idea of my mother as some knight's lady love took my breath away. Her lover was Sir Lamorak, my aunt said, son of that old rogue Pellinore, now dead.

"But—but why?" I blurted like a child. "Did he seduce her?" I felt that he might have done so as a way of avenging his father.

Morgan le Fay lifted her goblet of wine in her plump hand and laughed at me heartily. "No, I think not," she said when she could speak. "More likely the reverse. Morgause has always liked her men young and royal." She winked at me.

She was saying—she was saying that Morgause had seduced King Arthur? But then he was not so much to blame, and Morgause could have showed me more of the warmth of a mother, I thought, feeling my heart congeal into anger. Once I had pitied her, but not anymore.

"She has put off her wimple, then?" I tried to match my aunt Morgan's light tone, and perhaps I succeeded. She laughed.

"Indeed, yes, she has put off her wimple. Now she wears her hair in a jeweled caul of gold." Morgan le Fay waited while a servant brought in the meat—squab, rabbit pie, roast suckling pork—then added, seemingly as an afterthought, "Your brothers will murder her, of course. They will kill either her, or young Lamorak, or both."

I sat once more struggling for breath, partly because Morgan le Fay could speak so coolly of her sister's death while reaching for the rabbit pie, but mostly because—

I managed to speak. "You know the future?"

She gave me a glance as offhand as fate. Her eyes were brown, I noticed, dark—I was startled by the depth of their darkness in her round, powdered face. She said merely, "Sometimes."

"You are a seeress."

She shrugged. "Sometimes I see the workings of fate. Sometimes not. Eat your squab, Mordred, before it gets cold."

I did not eat my squab. I said, "In the Forest Perilous, I met three strange personages beneath an ash tree as big as the world." I told her of the three witches tending the brightly colored thread, the venerable crone and the maiden and the small girl with the shears.

Morgan's eyes grew round. "You're honored, Mordred." She regarded me with a sort of respect. "You are quite a personage, it seems. And you have the gift of scrying, yet. What a pity you were not born female. You would have made a mighty sorceress."

I shrugged. I had tried no scrying since I had learned it was the magic of ladies and matrons, those who have no power but to know secrets. Folk called me a coward; I did not want them calling me a woman.

"The one who cradled the thread invited me to draw my sword and cut it," I said. "I should have done so. I could have chosen for myself a long, long life."

Morgan le Fay shook her head. "Had you drawn your sword, you would have severed the thread in the exact same place as if it were cut by the heedless little girl."

I stared. "How can you say that?"

"Because that is the way fate works."

The servants brought bowls of strawberries, but for once Morgan le Fay seemed uninterested in eating. She leaned toward me in the candlelight and told me a story. There was once a knight, she said, and the king, his liege, had gifted him royally with a goblet fit for a prince, a great heavy vessel of pure gold. But when his lady saw the goblet, she turned white as a lily. Throw it in the river, she said. Bury it, burn it, put it away from you. It is your death. But the knight would not give up the king's gift. So as he slept, his lady crept out of their bedchamber and stole the goblet and hid it until she could think how to destroy it. When the knight awoke in the morning and saw that the goblet was gone, he was mightily enraged. Where have you put it? he roared at his lady. And when she would not answer him, he struck her so hard that she stumbled and fell against a doorway. And the goblet, which she had placed in a high niche above the doorway, fell down upon the knight's head, killing him.

"You see," said Morgan le Fay, "by trying to prevent fate, the lady actually aided it."

"Still," I said, "the knight could have chosen not to keep the goblet or strike the lady." It was late. Under the table

Gull slept. The candles had burned down and were trickling runnels of wax at first limpid like tears but then like cream and then flat white like the blind harper's eyes. I felt the wine buzzing in my head like bumblebees, like arrows shot to try to kill me, and in a kind of trance I watched the candles dripping.

"He could have," said Morgan le Fay, "but then his fate would have found him in a different way."

"But if that is so, then what is the use of even trying to do right?"

"What, indeed?" She leaned toward me with glittering eyes. "I will tell you another tale to show you the power of fate," she said. "Once there was a King who was seduced into fathering a baby by his own sister. And he knew that he was fated to be killed by this unnatural son. So he took all the boy babies in the kingdom, forty boy babies in all, and he put them all in a boat and gave them to the sea. And all those babies starved or died of cold or were drowned— except one."

"Me," I said. I spoke without raising my eyes from the tears of the candles, but my heart was pounding.

"And the one who survived was his son, who was destined to destroy him," said Morgan le Fay. "Do you see? There is no escaping the working of fate."

I said nothing, because for the first time the matter of the forty babies was making sense to me, in a hideous way: Maybe Merlin knew that one would survive and that it would be I, Mordred. Maybe that was why he told Arthur to do this evil thing, to send forty babes out to sea. Maybe it was not because fate could be defied, as Nyneve thought. Rather, it was only to show fate's awful power.

Maybe things were working out exactly as Merlin intended.

I said, "But suppose that the unnatural son decides he does not want to kill his father?" My voice did not come out as strongly as I would have liked.

"Ah," said Morgan le Fay, "fate would find a way. But as it happens, the son hates the father." My body clenched, and I would not let her look into my eyes. "By trying to kill him when he was a helpless baby, his father has given him reason to hate him," she went on. "Also, his father, the King, is so *noble*—" Somehow she made being noble sound like a dirty thing. "His father, the True King, is so noble that he is determined to accept his punishment. He will do nothing to prevent it."

Yes, he was noble, King Arthur. I wished I were half as noble. Anytime in the past nine years that he knew I was alive he could have killed me. Thinking of my sire, of his goodliness, gave me the courage to lift my gaze to meet Morgan's, and the bitterness in her dark, glittering eyes frightened me.

"He is your brother," I whispered. "Why do you wish him ill?"

"Like you, I have reason." She looked at me levelly, like a comrade. "Mordred, you are not alone."

My heart lurched, for of all things about being who I was, that was the one I found hardest to bear: feeling so much alone.

She poured me more wine. She said, "I will help you. Let us lay plans; let us take the throne together. By right it is doubly yours: You are the son, and you are the sister-son more truly than Gawain is."

True. I had thought so myself sometimes. And hated myself for the thought.

My aunt Morgan was watching me steadily. "We are much alike," she said. "I think we could share a throne. I think we would get along, Mordred, my young sorcerer."

But she barely knew me.

Yet she knew me all too well. She knew things she could not know merely by spying on me with her scrying mirror, the way she spied on her sister, Morgause. She seemed to know my soul.

Facing her was worse than facing ten knights in full armor. My heart pounded with dread, my head pounded so painfully I could not think, and everything she had said hung on me like robes of lead. And all, all of it felt true, and what was the bloody use of trying to do good, to be something more than this villain Mordred? It took my deepest courage just to speak in a wavering whisper.

"I want to try to do what is right." I took the wine she had given me and poured it onto the floor. "I want to fight my fate."

She blinked at me as if she heard a fly buzzing, as if I were not even worth swatting. She said to me as indifferently as if we were talking about the weather, "Stay with me a few days and you will think otherwise."

10

AFTER ONLY A FEW HOURS OF SLEEP IN MY SUMPTUOUS chamber, I groaned and awoke, as I had commanded myself to do. I would dress and arm myself, I planned, then go to the stable while it was still dark and no one would see me. I would saddle my horse. The gate would open at first light, and I would ride like a hawk on the wind; I would be miles away before Morgan le Fay called for me.

I had done well to face her, I told myself, and I had learned much. Now I knew what was her game.

Yet I struggled to buckle on my sword. Mere fear had never made me so weak. Yes, there had been some threat in her tone toward the end. But threats had never made me want to lie down and sleep forever.

It was hard even to set one foot in front of the other, to walk. But I had to do it. "Gull," I whispered, and she padded over to me, and with her following like a white shadow at my heels I walked softly out of my chamber and down the tower stairs.

Down, down the dark spiral staircase, one hand on the damp stone, feeling my way. The walls were cold and smelled of moss. It seemed to take forever to reach the door at the bottom where I would let myself out and cross the courtyard to the stable.

Finally the stairs ended. There, at last, the door—

I opened it and looked in upon my own chamber.

But it was impossible.

But it was so. There stood the candle by which I had dressed. There was my bed as I had left it, with the linens thrown back. There on their perches stood the caged birds, their heads under their wings.

"Gull," I whispered, "I am going insane." I closed the chamber door and stood outside it, feeling earth under my feet; I was at the base of the tower, and stairs led only upward from here. "Very well," I muttered, and I started to climb.

Halfway up the tower was a door that led to a walkway on top of a connecting wall. Fumbling in the darkness, I found that door. I opened it.

My chamber again.

It could not be. The door led through the outer wall of the tower.

Pressing against my legs, Gull shivered and whined as if she heard thunder.

I had not the strength even to pat her. I thought of walking into the chamber, proving it was an illusion, walking through the far wall—but what if I missed the path, what if I stepped out on air? I sank down, sat on the floor and stared.

118

After a while I struggled up again and made my way back to my chamber.

It was still there.

I let my helm, my sword, and my chain mail fall to the floor. In my fine new clothing I lay in the bed, but although I felt weary enough to die, I could not sleep.

First light dawned, then full light, then sunrise, and I lay there. A servant came and told me, "My lady requests the favor of your company at breakfast, Sir Mordred."

The servant led the way; I followed. This time the doorways led to Morgan le Fay.

Our small, private table was set up in her solarium. I sat without speaking, and the servant brought what should have been a treat for me: kippered herring. But I did not eat.

"So, Mordred," said Morgan le Fay, as plump and cheery as a sparrow, "you are learning."

I said nothing.

"Such is the nature of fate," she told me. "You try this way and that way, but you arrive at the same end."

"Such is the nature of sorcery," I said, trying to leash the anger in my voice.

"Nay! Not so." Morgan le Fay rose to stand over me. "There is no mere magic here. This castle is my bones, my self, and I—do you not understand who I am? In druid days they called me The Fate Morgana. Before that, the goddess of doom, Morrigan. Take heed to the things I tell you, son of Morgause. I know of what I speak."

I sensed by the prickling in my marrow that she spoke truth, and I knew the name of the feeling that made me deadly weak; it was more than fear. It was despair.

She spoke truth—yet she wanted me to rush fate, kill Arthur tomorrow if not today, put her on the throne with me—was that her destiny? Odd that Merlin had not mentioned her in his prophecies.

Anger helped me somewhat. I stood up, taller than she. "I am leaving now," I said, and I turned my back and walked away from her.

I knew the way to the courtyard—down the tower, then through a corridor to the great hall, then out. With Gull at my heels I descended the tower steps and opened the door.

It led into my chamber, of course.

I stepped into the—chamber, illusion, whatever it might be—and closed the door behind me. I no longer cared that it could not be real. I tested the walls with my hand; the stone felt solid. I opened one of the mullioned windows and looked out. Where there should have been a corridor I saw the view from my tower chamber, a hundred feet of steep stone and then the chasm and the fierce river foaming white over hidden boulders. I closed the window and pounded the bed with my fist. I hated this room now, hated it, this fine lofty bedchamber that had once seemed so welcoming to me. Overhead in their cages the linnets and partridges were singing. How could they sing? They were prisoners, trapped as surely as I was. I seized the basin from the washstand and hurled it through a window, shattering the glass. Anger helped. I stood on the bed and reached up, and then I piled pillows on the bed and stood on them and tried again, trying to pull down the cages and release the birds so that they, at least, could fly out the window and be free. But I could not reach them.

I stumbled off the bed and dropped to my knees on the floor beside Gull. I took her head between my faltering hands. Her brown eyes looked back at me gravely.

"Nyneve," I whispered to Gull's eyes, "help me."

Time passed. Maybe a few moments, maybe a few hours. I do not know. I gazed without blinking into Gull's sober brown eyes, and Gull sat as still as ladywater with her head between my hands, gazing back at me.

"Nyneve. Please, help."

She was far away, as far from me as Pelleas had quested far from her. But slowly I reached her. I saw the shadowy green water first, and then the lilies floating on the still surface, yellow, creamy white. And then Nyneve, sitting alone and pensive in a vine-clad arbor half veiled by willows on the island shore.

"Nyneve!" I cried.

She turned, startled, and her sweet voice sounded inside my head. *Mordred?*

I was not close enough to see her face. Even so, my throat closed; I could not speak.

Mordred? Is something wrong? What is it?

I made myself speak. "Trapped in Caer Morgana," I whispered.

I see. She did see me now, somehow. I have never understood how Nyneve scried in air, but somehow she had drawn me closer. I could see her face—thinner since I had seen her last, too thin—and I watched as her wise eyes studied my despair, and considered it, and made a decision. *Follow Gull,* she said.

"Gull is as frightened as I am."

I am speeding to you by the soul ways; I will enter into her. Follow her. Nyneve blinked, and it was as if a strong wind had whitened the surface of still water; I could see her no more.

Gull stood up, shook herself, and looked at me.

"Wait a moment," I told her. I armed myself—mail, helm, shield, sword—for I did not know what danger I might meet. "Very well," I told my noble brachet, "lead on."

She took me straight through the wall.

Through the wall of my chamber, walking where I had seen nothing but air and the sickening drop into the chasm and the river. I gulped and followed. Her passing had softened the stone somehow. I walked through it as if tearing through gray wool, and on the other side—

On the other side, I was in my chamber again, with Gull waiting for me.

"Bloody hell," I grumbled as she led off in a different direction. I followed.

Through the wall. Into my loathesome bedchamber yet again. And through the wall once more, and—still in that same hateful, fateful room. I appealed to Gull, "When will this end?"

Be careful what you wish for, folk say; you might get it. I wanted something different to happen, anything, and something did. I heard shouts—"Stop him! To horse!" Gull took off at a run, and I ran after her. Through the wall and through the wall and through the wall—I drew my sword and hacked at the accursed thing. The shouts sounded closer behind us, and I heard thudding hooves. Through the wall again—

Falling.

I ran forward and then I was falling through the floor and then it was as if the gray fabric of the fate or the enchantment, call it what you will, as if the gray stone walls shredded into long ribbons of mist trailing down the rocks of the abyss as I fell into it. I glimpsed armed riders along the cliff top, and then—I hope I did not scream—rocks blurred past me. I think I hit the water before I had time to scream.

Rushing, foaming water. Swift and deep.

Then I knew almost with joy that fate was a liar; King Arthur would live long and I would die very shortly. I would drown.

In that torrent up was down and down was up and the water surged and snarled and chivvied me along like a flood of gray wolves, all was dark and white, I breathed water, I could not have screamed if I tried, I was dying, I did not want to die, my hands thrashed and flailed—and one of them came down on something warm and slippery and alive.

Gull.

With one hand on her back I hoisted my head above water. I gasped for breath, choked, coughed, gasped again. At some time since I had fallen from the top of the cliff I had lost my sword, my shield, and my helm; now I tore off my heavy chain mail as well and kicked off my boots. I could breathe. I might live. Gull paddled strongly, riding the water like a little white boat, and the swift water whirled us along between steep stony banks, away from Caer Morgana, until the ravine opened into a valley dense with forest on both sides, and the water quieted, and Gull paddled us to shore.

I crawled out of the water, lay on mud, and coughed until I vomited.

When I could sit up, I looked at Gull, who lay panting beside me. I had nothing but the soaked clothing on my body, but I was alive. "Thank you," I told her.

I hoped Nyneve could hear me, but knew that probably she could not. Probably she was already gone. Humbly I sensed how hard it was, hard and dangerous, for her to be in Gull in that way.

She had looked as if she were in a bad way. I knew that, quest or no quest, I must go to her.

In a pavilion in the Forest Perilous, a knight lay sleeping in his smallclothes, his naked sword near his hand. The first glimmer of dawn gave enough light. I crept in silently in my bare feet, but once I held the sword in my hand, I smacked him across the chest with the flat of it to awaken him.

He reared up with a roar, "Thief!" But I addressed him with the sword to silence him.

"I am going to take your armor and your sword," I told him, "and your lance and your horse, for I have need of them."

He turned a rich shade of red, like the wild strawberries that dotted the meadows.

"But you can fight me for them, if you like," I added cheerfully. "Do you have an extra sword?"

I stepped back, and he bolted for a weapon—and a shield,

while I had nothing but my tunic wrapped around my fore-arm—and then he lunged at me.

Odd, what a difference a few days had made. He was stronger than I, but my despair had hardened in me, and I did not care whether I were killed; if I died, very well, it would spite Morgan le Fay and prove her wrong. Reckless, I took cuts yet fought like a very demon, quick and hungry. In only a few moments I forced him to the ground.

"Yield," I told him, the point of my sword at his throat.

He glared up at me. "Curse you."

"I am already well accursed. Say that you yield."

"I yield."

"Your name?"

"Sir Dalbert."

I let him up and went about taking what I needed. I packed his saddlebags with half his provisions, leaving him the rest, and I saddled his horse. I put on his boots—he was only a little larger than I; I had chosen him for size. I put on his chain mail, his breastplate and visored helm, and tasse and cuisses and greaves and gauntlets. I slung on his sword and shield as he watched me with tight-lipped hatred. I selected a lance. Once fully armed, I could not mount the horse. I needed a squire and wondered whether Sir Dalbert would serve. "Help me mount," I ordered him, and I purposefully turned my back on him.

He ran at me, holding the other sword like a spear to pierce my mail. I sidestepped, turned at the same time, drew my sword and lopped off the top of his head.

It was the first time I had killed a man.

The gore made me retch. Other than that, I felt nothing for him. My left arm and shoulder hurt like fire from the cuts he had given me, and I was glad he was dead.

Perhaps I would be more like Gawain now that I had killed a knight.

I put off his armor except for mail, breastplate, helm, and greaves, and I mounted his charger—my charger now. My armor, although the shield bore his device—quarterly red and gold, with three black eagles.

Many foes recognized it, I found as I rode. "Sir Dalbert! You renegade, you killed my brother!" "Sir Dalbert! Traitor knight, defend yourself!" And they would charge me. Some I fought. Most I fled. Let them call Sir Dalbert a coward for a change.

"The first village I find," I told Gull as she trotted by my side, "I will get something to paint out this Dalbert's device."

This started me thinking of what my own device might be, now that I was a full knight, for I would not claim the device of Lothian.

"A white brachet in a green field—make that a field of daisies. A white brachet lying in the daisies, *couchant*, with ears rampant," I teased.

She merely trotted, panting happily.

As it turned out, I traded a brace of hares to an old charcoal burner for a bucket of limewash, and I painted my shield with it. So with a shield argent—white—as if I were yet a virgin knight, I rode on toward Avalon.

When I thought of Nyneve, her face too thin, I rode faster.

11

EVEN AT THE HEIGHT OF SUMMER, THE LAND LAY LUSH AND green—thank the goodliness of our blessed King Arthur.

I rode westward, trusting Gull to find Avalon for me, and I met many folk, but only one whom I remember well.

She rode westward also, on a roan palfrey, and I overtook her on the trail. As I turned to greet her, I knew her. It was the damsel who had appealed to me over the body of her dead brother.

I reined in my charger to ride beside her, for only if a woman were a sorceress like Nyneve could she safely ride forth by herself. "Maiden, why do you travel alone?"

"You!" She turned on me, eyes like blue fire. But as I raised my visor, her eyes widened; she remembered my face, and it was not the face she expected in that helm. "You?" I saw her glance at my shield—Sir Dalbert's device still showed faintly through the whitewash—and at Gull. Then she regarded me gravely. "Is that a sword cut on your cheekbone? It seems you have avenged my brother after all."

"I—I am sorry." About her brother, I meant. And sorry that I had ridden past her and left her sorrowing over his body.

"Do not be sorry. You wear the armor of that ruffian Sir Dalbert; you have killed him, have you not?"

"Yes."

"Then do not be sorry for anything. What is your name?"

"What is yours?"

"Lynette. But I asked first."

I smiled. Some serene lilt in her voice made me wish to be mysterious. "Call me the Knight of the White Brachet." I was flirting, though I barely knew how.

She laughed, a sweet sound; I was happy to have made her laugh. "The Knight of the White Brachet! That's an odd sort of title for a warrior."

"I am an odd sort of warrior."

We rode together and talked. She told me that her brother and three retainers had ridden with her when she left home, but the retainers had deserted her after her brother was killed. Once she had seen him buried, she had thought of turning back—her home was in Caer Sarsen, far to the east—but her pride made her go on. She was journeying to Tintagel, she told me, to be a lady companion for Queen Morgause.

"For—for Queen Morgause?" The Knight of the White Brachet, of course, could not reveal himself by saying that Queen Morgause was his mother. Moreover, I found myself still dismayed by what Morgan le Fay had told me—my mother, dallying?—and my troubled feelings kept me silent. I said only, "I thought Queen Morgause lived in Lothian."

"Yes, but she has traveled to Tintagel to be with Sir Lamorak. He is a knight of the Round Table. Do you know him?" Lynette asked, all innocence. The minx, she was trying to find out who I was.

"Do *you* know him?"

"I asked first."

"And what if I do not answer?"

"Then you must perform a task for me." Her smile, coy, told me that it would be no ordinary knightly task.

She made me dismount from my tall charger and pluck her a bouquet of buttercups. Over the next five days, traveling with her, I performed many such tasks for her because I would not tell her my name or whom I served. She made me gather strawberries for her to eat, find her a four-leafed clover, capture a butterfly for her to wear in her hair—and I did it all gladly. Being with her made me more lighthearted than I had been since I was a child. I would have done far more than chase butterflies for her—and I did; twice I had to fight for her, jousting with knights who challenged me for her as offhandedly as if she were a horse they fancied. Each time I met the challenger even though he was more heavily armed and armored than I. Each time I took a lance on my breastplate but managed somehow to keep my feet in the stirrups, and each time on the second challenge I unhorsed the challenger. Feeling Lynette's gaze upon me made me able to do this, and to fight on with the sword, and to bear the blows and the pain, compelling my opponent to yield.

I escorted Lynette safely to the gates of Tintagel, and there I took my leave of her.

"But will you not come within?" Her sky-blue gaze—I could barely withstand it. "Come, my bold knight, your wounds need time to heal. Come in, rest for a few days."

"I cannot." It had been almost two years since I had seen my lady mother, but after the news I had heard of her, I wished to make it more years, many more. I did not think I could courteously give her greeting. "I must go," I told Lynette. "I have a quest I must fulfill." This was true, but I made it sound mysterious, as befitted the Knight of the White Brachet.

Lynette studied me, her blue eyes misty with pity. "You are a knight-errant, are you not? Have you no family, no comrades? You ride all alone."

"I have Gull."

"But you said you have no one to avenge you if you were killed."

She remembered. Even though she had been grieving for her brother the moment we first met, she remembered what I had said. My heart bounded, so that I could barely speak. "I must go," I murmured, and I lifted her hand to my lips and kissed it.

Then I rode away. My heart ached, yet at the same time swelled with joy to feel her looking after me.

Avalon.

It was not a castle. There was no castle anywhere, not even a tower keep. How this could be, when I had seen Nyneve and Pelleas sitting in a solarium there, I did not understand, but perhaps scrying showed things differently.

Avalon was a lake. A great, still, indigo-green lake spotted with water lilies. Swans glided there, black, white, dusky blue, one with a red breast. Herons waded there, gray, white, spangled, standing like wizards in the shadows of the willow islands, their golden eyes glinting. Swallows flitted down like sunbeams and skimmed the water. Speckled fish lazed at the surface, and turtles floated like the lily pads.

I came to Avalon an hour before sunset. At the edge of that lake, Gull lay down as if at a hearth. And out of nowhere came a lad who led my horse away as if to stabling, although I saw no stabling. So I laid aside my helm and shield, sat on the feathery grass of the shore and waited.

In the silver-gold hour after sundown, I heard the sounds of harp music and maidens singing. Then six maidens came poling a shallow boat between the lilies, laughing, their feet bare, their gowns flowing like water, their hair flowing and unbound. When they saw me sitting on the shore, they grew silent and guided the boat toward me. We stepped on board, Gull and I, and the maidens took us a winding way between a maze of small islands where owls watched from the willow trees. It was nightfall when we neared a torchlit place that might have been a larger island or Avalon's far shore or the green brow of a giant sleeping under all that water.

Or the land of the ever young, for I saw no one old there. Young harpers sat cross-legged upon the quay where the maidens docked the barge, playing merrily and singing. Many maidens clustered around them, maidens as fair as honey roses, laughing as sweetly as the harpers sang. The music called to me, as music always did; I would have liked to stay and watch and listen for a while. But with ears flying, Gull ran into the shadows, baying a brachet song of gladness, and I followed.

The lake glimmered under moonlight now. In her arbor by the shore sat Nyneve, all alone except for the white falcon on her shoulder.

The white falcon? But then—where was Pelleas?

Gull stood with her head pressed against Nyneve's knee, whining.

I walked slowly into the arbor. "Nyneve?"

Patting Gull, she turned to me and smiled, but the smile did not ripple the stillness of her eyes, and her face was so thin and pale that, instead of bowing to her, I bent and kissed her on the side of her beautiful head. I had never done such a thing before.

I sat with her. "What has happened to him?"

"I—I am not sure." She shifted on her wicker bench to face me. "It happened while I was with you and my body was sitting here, so I do not know. I came back, and . . ." Her hand floated up, white in the night, to caress the falcon. "And here she was."

There had been no hint of blame in what she said, yet I felt keenly to blame.

"I cannot think he is dead," Nyneve said almost in a whisper. "I *do* not think he is dead." Her voice grew stronger. "I would know if he were dead. I would feel it."

"You—perhaps he sensed . . ." I stumbled over this, it was all so strange to me. "You were in danger, helping me. . . ."

"He sent the falcon back to me? Perhaps." I could tell she

did not think so. She looked away from me, far away, as her fingers stroked the bird's shoulder. "She flew far; she was very worn and tired. She is stronger now, and each day she flies out longer. Soon I will send her looking for him."

"You cannot see . . ."

"Scrying?" She shook her head. "No, I can see nothing. Do you know what I think, Mordred?" I could scarcely believe it, how her warm voice greeted me as an old friend, how her warm glance embraced me. "I think he has fulfilled his quest. I think that he has found the Grail, and finding it has transported him so far from here that he does not remember me."

Let her think what she chose if it helped her. "But he will return," I said.

"I think so. Yes."

"I dreamed of him finding the Grail!" Suddenly I remembered. "Before I left Camelot."

I told her of my vision in which Pelleas had laid his naked sword across the throats of the two sleepers, Gawain and the maiden. Nyneve smiled with wonder. "But that happened long ago!" Pelleas had been in love with the maiden, but she scorned him, and Gawain had offered to persuade her on Pelleas's behalf. Then he had seduced her for himself. Pelleas had spared his life and hers, but he had never forgiven him. "It was how we met," Nyneve said softly. Pelleas had been ready to kill himself when Nyneve had taken away his pain with her magical hands.

Nyneve's smile rippled away, and she stared at me. "But you say that in your vision he found the Grail?"

"A cauldron of blood."

"What is the matter?" she asked me. I suppose my face had changed.

So much blood. Too much blood in a man. "Nyneve," I questioned her abruptly, "what is the meaning of the white stag that flees and flees with the black hounds panting always at its heels?"

A few heartbeats fled before she answered. "The King," she said softly. "The white deer is King Arthur."

"And the hounds," I said, "are everything that would destroy him."

"Yes."

Including the stubborn resentment in me. I did not tell Nyneve this, for I would no longer be a child and tell her everything; I was a knight now and I would find my own way. I asked her, "Why does Morgan le Fay wish him dead?"

She sighed and leaned toward the lake, laying her head against a pillar, her face in shadow. She said, "I have told you it is a hard thing to be a woman. Morgan le Fay is one who could have been our blessed liege King Morgan had she only been born a man."

"And I could have been an eagle to fly away from here had I only been born with wings."

Nyneve sat up and scowled at me. "You of all men should understand. You have felt yourself to be a chattel of your so-called fate; is not a woman a chattel of her low estate? Morgan le Fay rules her lands as ably as any lord in the realm, but King Arthur will not title her or admit her to his council."

But King Arthur was right. The idea of titling a woman

was laughable. "Why, what would he call her? Lord Morgan?"

Nyneve did not answer, but merely gazed at me levelly and asked, "Have you found that for which you quest?"

She stopped my laughter in my throat. How did she know of my quest? And what was she trying to tell me?

"No," I replied, feeling fear coil in the hollow of my chest, "I have found nothing." Speaking with my fisherfather had not helped me. Speaking with Morgan le Fay had only made things worse. I felt my fate riding like a serpent on my shoulders, winding tighter around me day by day.

"And for what did you come here? To speak with me?"

I understood her then. She was saying that I needed her—a woman—to be my ally. She angered me, but I saw the falcon on her shoulder and pitied her, so I said nothing of my anger. "I came to thank you for saving my life," I told her quietly, "and to see if you are all right."

That surprised a soft sound out of her, a sigh that might almost have been a sob. After a moment she said with something of her old gentle merriment, "You're welcome. And what will you do about it if I am not all right?"

"I don't know."

"Dear Mordred." She had never spoken to me so tenderly. "There is nothing you can do. But since you are here, you should seek audience with the Lady of the Lake. Perhaps she can help you find what you are seeking."

I slept that night in an airy pavilion on Avalon shore, and the next day the maidens fed me flowers by the plateful, amaranth and lilies and columbine and asphodel. It seemed not at all odd to eat flowers. In that one day my wounds healed as if they had never been. Then I slept again in the pavilion with Gull by my side.

In the afternoon of the next day, Nyneve came for me. "Are you ready?"

I stood up and buckled on my sword so as to appear before the Lady of the Lake as a knight and a warrior. But Nyneve stood smiling—I remembered that selfsame smile from when she had first greeted me, nearly ten years before—and shaking her head at me.

"Mordred," she said, "you'd do better to put that aside, with your shield and helm and mail. Better to put off your boots and spurs too."

"And go barefoot?"

"Assuredly. Don't you remember? We took away all those toys once before, ladywater and I, in the river below Caer Morgana."

I stood with my hand on my sword hilt, my mouth sagging open, gawking at her.

She said, "What made you in such a hurry to take up arms again? Or ever? You could have been once more a carefree churl, a lad with a little white dog, both of you lying in the sun. You could have gone off and picked wild cherries. You could have built yourself a hut and lived there and been a woodcutter, and Gull could have caught you rabbits to eat. Why didn't you?"

Such thoughts had never occurred to me. It made my heart ache that they had not, but I firmed my mouth and let my face show her nothing. "I'm a true noble, as you once said."

"Yes, and that little X behind your ear, it is a dark, dark bird flying lower every day. Put off your boots and your sword if you wish to speak with my liege lady."

I did so, and followed her to the verge of the lake. Very still, the water gleamed a deep, glassy green in the morning light. Lilies floated with their yellow throats open to the sky, their petals stark white against the dark water and the velvet-green lily pads. I saw no castle, no court, no lady.

I looked around. "Where is she?"

"She is everywhere. To speak with her, you must go to sleep in the lake."

12

THE MAIDENS WERE LAUGHING AT ME, SPLASHES OF LAUGH-
ter, melodious, like the giggling of a fountain. "You must
trust us," said the maiden at my head, her words a warm
breath in my ear. "Look, you lie as rigid as a sword. Loosen
your arms." But I could not yet loosen my arms, which were
crossed on my chest. I lay upon the water of the great lake,
on my back, facing the sky, in danger of sinking, and sur-
rounding me head to toe stood the damsels of Avalon, their
gowns flowing and floating around them, their faces clustered like lilies, their arms supporting me. I was to sleep this
night on a limpid, rippling, insubstantial bed. Like Fisherfather's frail coracle bobbing on the vast chest of old Lyr, I lay
on the warm bosom of ladywater—warm and pleasant and
terrifying. If I wished to speak with the Lady, I had to do this
thing, and if her damsels betrayed me, I would drown.

"Trust us," said the maiden softly again.

But—what if they got tired and let me go? What if they

talked with one another and forgot to watch my breathing? What if I rolled over in my sleep and they were not strong enough to stop me? Trust them? This was the most difficult of all tasks the Lady could have given me.

I closed my eyes against the brightness of the sky and decided to get through it as quickly as I could.

Nevertheless, it took hours. I tried not to think of how it had felt to breathe water, to gasp and choke and nearly drown in water stronger than a giant's fist. I thought about it anyway. I opened my eyes to look straight up at a sky tawny with sundown, and again to look up at stars. I began to grow so weary of my own fear that I relaxed. After that— it seemed to me that I opened my eyes again and looked, but at last I must have been asleep, for I was looking into a darkly sparkling indigo-green face, a lovely, maidenly face with great eyes that opened and opened and swirled and swam and floated like water lilies.

It was Nyneve—yet it was not Nyneve; it was more than Nyneve. It was Guinevere before she met Arthur or Lancelot, it was Lynette, it was every white-armed damsel anywhere, it was Morgan le Fay before she learned to hate, it was my mother Morgause when she was a fair young woman setting off to Camelot. She, the one I faced, she was the maiden of all maidens. Yet she was more than that. I do not know how to say what she was, the Lady of the Lake.

"Lady Vivien," I whispered. Lady of life.

Lying upon ladywater, gazing into the depths of Avalon, I spread my arms upon the surface, trying to embrace that lady's greatness, her vastness. The maidens had long since left me; on my own I slept on the lake, floating on the bosom of the lady, lazily swimming in water as warm as my own blood's pulsing, and I did not drown.

"Lady of Avalon," I addressed her, "I am Mordred."

She smiled, a rippling, shimmering smile like moonlight silvering her darkness. It was as if she knew my name—she who had given King Arthur his sword Excalibur, very likely she knew my name and all about me, very likely she knew more than Merlin did, but her own knowledge was not important to her. A starling in the sky was more important.

As if I had already explained everything to her just by telling her my name, as if I had told her the whole problem, I begged, "Teach me how to fight my fate."

Her moon-shadow smile broadened. She did not speak, but in that moment I knew, I understood, it all seemed so simple. I did not need sword and shield and armor for this quest; I did not need to fight. I needed only to live. Just to be, like a swallow on the wing or a turtle sunning. Just to be happy.

As if some great and shining fish had jumped, the lady rippled and glistened; now her eyes were silver rings. And she spoke to me, a single word: *Love.*

The next morning I took gentle leave of Nyneve. "He will come back to you," I told her.

She looked up at the white falcon flying far overhead and nodded. "I hope so."

"He will."

She said, "I wish I bore his baby."

I opened my mouth, then shut it again; there was nothing fitting that I could say. Why did she not bear his baby? Perhaps she needed the King's healing?

"I am a sorceress," Nyneve said, seeing my confusion. "It is within my power to decide whether to bear a child, and now I wish that I had decided differently. His baby—I would have had something of him. Now I have nothing."

Urgently, urgently I felt what it could be to have a sweetheart, how sad to have none. I kissed Nyneve and rode away, spurring my steed into a gallop as soon as I was out of her sight. At reckless speed I rode toward Tintagel, where Lynette, please whatever fey god took charge of these things, where Lynette might yet await me.

Love, the Lady of Avalon had said to me.

With Lynette I had been happy. For those few days of riding with her, my burden of fate had lifted from me as if it had never been. If she would be my lady love . . . if this blessing could be, then King Arthur would live to be old and die in his bed. I would put away my sword and spend my days sweetly in love with Lynette.

Well rested, my horse ran willingly. Gull ran happily beside me, her tail cutting a white smile in the air; when she grew tired, I carried her on the saddle before me. Knights challenged me; I declined them and galloped by. I was no longer afraid of being called a coward.

In a mere three days, as quickly as the steed could carry me, I cantered up to the gates of Tintagel, amid the roar of the sea crashing on the sea cliffs below the towers.

I got there just at sunset. The portcullis was being cranked down, but the guards halted it for the sake of the bold Knight of the White Brachet.

Two other knights arrived just as I did and rode in with me, fine strong knights in handsome armor. Their horses shone as if they had ridden but a short distance, even though it was late in the day. They bore shields argent, a canton gules, with eagles: the device of Lothian.

"Well, Gawain, my brother, and Garet," I greeted them.

In their helms they turned as if they were hooded hawks, lifting their visors to stare at me. They had taken me for a weary old knight-errant in hacked and battered armor, but now they saw that I carried Gull in my arms.

"Mordred?" Garet sounded incredulous.

I lifted my visor so that they could see my face.

Garet stared. "You're scarred. Have you finally learned to fight, then?"

Before I could answer, or think of an answer, Gawain began to laugh. "Mordred! Have you come to visit our lady mother?"

"Yes," I said, which was partly true; I knew I would not be able to avoid her.

"Well met! Our lady mother seems much courted these days. We must visit her together." He rode across the inner ward to the keep, where he dismounted, but instead of sending his horse to the stable he told the boy to hold it for him. Garet did likewise. I wondered why, but did not ask. My thoughts were all for my lady love as I sent my weary steed to the stable and followed Gawain and Garet into the great hall with Gull trotting behind me.

Folk sat at long tables eating their supper. Scanning the room, I did not see Lynette. I looked to the dais, where she might have been waiting upon my lady mother, but Queen Morgause must have been taking her meal elsewhere; no one sat upon the dais but—I blinked; it was the blind harper I remembered from my first day in Camelot, the ancient white-eyed harper in a rough dark robe, with the raven perched on his shoulder. He lifted his harp to play, but the raven swung its heavy head toward me. "Dread!" it cried. "More dread!"

I felt its words strike cold against my chest, but folk only laughed, grinning at me and Gawain and Garet, the newcomers; it was just the bird's joke. We were knights, after all. We had killed people. But now we would sit down and eat. Would we not?

Gull lifted her nose longingly toward the scent of food, but my brothers passed straight through the great hall, and I followed. Gawain and Garet seemed to know their way somehow. They walked rapidly along a corridor, up a spiral stairway, and along a corridor again to the great oak door at the end. Before the doorway stood a maiden. When I saw her, my heart beat like dove wings, for it was Lynette.

As Gawain and Garet strode toward her, she stepped forward courteously to meet them and stand in their way. "Good knights," she told them, "pardon, but you may not enter here."

"Surely our lady mother will be overjoyed to see us," said Gawain sardonically.

"No, I am sorry. Queen Morgause is—" Lynette interrupted herself with a gasp as she caught sight of me. Her lovely face flushed. Her wide, sky-hued eyes gazed at me, and I gazed at her.

As we stood staring, Gawain and Garet brushed past her, making toward the doorway. Lynette came to herself with a start. "No!" she cried after them.

"Brothers," I said, "wait!"

Gawain was trying the door, which was barred. Garet turned on me. "Still a coward, Mordred?"

He drew his sword, but he had already killed my hope, in that moment, as the sound of my name echoed between the stone walls of Tintagel. Hearing that name, Lynette paled corpse white and stumbled away from me, shaking. "Mordred?" Her voice was a shivering whisper, as if my face had turned to cancer.

I stretched one hand toward her in appeal. "Lynette, I—"

"Get away! You . . . you're the one they all talk about. Evil, unnatural—"

There was a clash of metal, then a rending of wood as Gawain and Garet broke down the door. Lynette cried out and darted after them to try to stop them as they dashed into the chamber with raised swords. How brave she was. I lunged forward and caught her around the waist, but I could barely hold her; she flailed wildly against me, terrified of my touch. "Don't! Please! Monster—"

From within the chamber came a woman's scream, a man's hoarse shout, and I was saying, "Don't, Lynette, they'll slay you too," and the woman in the chamber was crying out, "No! No, stop! Please—" and I was struggling with Lynette to pull her away from the shattered door, she screamed as if I were trying to hurt her, and from within the chamber came the wet *thwack* of swords hacking into flesh, and the man's shout gurgled away, and the woman's screams—I could not yet think of it as my mother screaming—the woman's screams gave way to sudden silence, cut off.

In the silence, footsteps echoed as folk came running from all directions, and someone was pommeling me to make me let go of Lynette, or perhaps Lynette was hitting me as she sobbed, "Monster, traitor, murderer," and I let her go. I strode away.

As I stumbled through the great hall, almost running, from the bard's shoulder the raven laughed at me—black, croaking laughter.

Outside the keep, I took Gawain's horse—no one tried to stop me—and I slashed the reins of the other horse, Garet's horse, and sent it skittering away. It was a small revenge, a pitiful revenge, for the bloody death of my hope.

Perhaps I should not have blamed Gawain and Garet. My lady love would have heard my name soon enough.

Oh, her white face. Horror, there had been nothing but horror for me in Lynette from the moment she learned that I was Mordred.

Because I am Mordred, she thought that I had been trying to ravish her. Lynette thought that I had been trying to carry her away.

I fought my way out of Tintagel by the postern gate, leaving two guards bleeding as I galloped off into the night. On a black horse I rode, and my fate coiled around my chest, tight, hurtfully tight, and hissed like storm wind in my ears. It was no use to fight it. It was no use. Whoever had said "love" to me was a fool; folk hated me even though I had done nothing evil except to be born.

I began to wonder what would happen to me after I killed King Arthur.

I was so in despair. Even Gull's faithfulness could not comfort me. When I finally halted the black horse that night, threw off my weapons and armor and lay on the dank grass of the Forest Perilous, my sweet little brachet pressed against me and licked my face, but I turned my face to the ground. I ached all over as if I had been in mortal combat, when all I had been fighting was—

My fate? *My* fate? King Arthur's fate. It was for his sake that I was locked in this losing battle, and no one cared. Even Merlin's prophecy took no account of me. After I killed King Arthur, would I live? Would I be King? Would I be a happy, blessed Liege King whose goodliness sustained the realm? It was not impossible. King Arthur had started off his reign with a bloody deed, and look at him, so golden, look how folk adored him. After I slew him, would they love me?

I wanted to kill myself for thinking it. His grave, noble face confronted me in the night as if in a scrying mirror, looking at me the way he had the day I had named my quest to him. The proud tilt of his jaw. His smile as he said to me, "Go with my blessing." The warm mist in his eyes.

I could not sleep.

I would die if fate made me kill him, I thought. Surely I would die. If not by the sword, then I would die of a broken heart.

Why would he not call me son? If only I were his son, I could be good.

Or if only I did not know I was his son. . . .

Damn everything. Damn that pompous old charlatan Merlin with his prophecies and his interference. If it were not for him—

I sat up as if to bay at the moon, my eyes wide. I stared, but I was not seeing the moonlight, the branches shifting and creaking in the wind, the lavender mushrooms glowing in the shadows.

Merlin. He was gone, but—but he was not dead. Through the rock in which he was imprisoned—or the tree, the glass hill, whatever, somewhere in Cornwall—one could still hear him pleading for freedom, legend said.

One could still speak with him.

13

I RODE THROUGH LANDS MORE STRANGE AND DAUNTING than any I had traversed before. No one challenged me, for no other knights rode there. In those western reaches of the Forest Perilous, great tors towered above the trees—they looked like ordinary mountains, yet just as I glanced away, the rocks would wink and grin. At night they roared and laughed. In the morning they might have moved slightly. On the tips of their crags teetered great boulders, some as large as a cottage, rocking as if they would fall. The trees moved when there was no wind. As I passed them, behind my back I would hear the sound of giggling.

I rode past a pile of glittering jewels each as large as my head; I did not dare to touch them, for they looked at me with dead eyes. I rode through a river that crackled like glass; Gull would not cross it until I carried her on the saddle before me. I rode under a willow tree that wept blood. I looked up, and there perched a great bird with the face of a fair, sorrowing woman, her long hair flowing down around her yellow, clawed feet.

I heard the music of a harp.

On the seventh day after I left hope behind me at Tintagel, I heard the music of a harp being played by a peerless harper. Never since I was a boy in Lothian and heard my first harper had the music echoed through me so. I heard no singing, no voices but the grunting of the tors, the tittering of the forest; it did not matter. Each note of the harp rang me as if I were riding inside a golden bell. That yearning music—it cried of mortal sorrow, yet by some glorious alchemy it turned sadness to surpassing joy. *Love, life, happiness, light after all,* the harp sang. The notes soared like larks, like eagles; even the trees listened. I shivered; it was like meeting the Grail.

I rode toward the sound of the music. I had to find the harper. I could not do otherwise.

There in the middle of the tangled wildwood grew a walled garden, like Queen Guinevere's garden in Camelot but not square; the stones and hedges of this wall stood in a great circle. I rode in—it was so great a garden that one could ride in on horseback. Roses grew as tall as trees there, and fruit trees interlaced like druid vine work into lattices and arches and pavilions, and yew bushes stood in shapes of peacocks, their tails bright with red and blue berries. Fountains of gold rose as tall as castle towers. In every way it was more splendid and fair than any garden I had seen or imagined. And over it all the sweetness of the harp music spread like the perfume of the roses, notes like petals falling.

149

Then, at the very center of the circular garden, I saw a great spiral cage standing. And in it, a hawk, playing with its beak upon the golden and silver wires that enclosed it as if upon the harp of Taliesin himself.

I had found the harper.

It was so humbling a marvel that I dismounted, and put aside my shield and helm, and left my horse behind. With Gull padding beside me I walked closer, gazing.

Intent upon his music, the hawk paid no attention to Gull and me. He was not hooded or leashed or belled, only caged as if he were a linnet, a starling—it had always hurt my heart to see the caged birds in gardens, imprisoned for the sake of their music, and the hawks standing blind and silent in the mews. It seemed somehow not only a hurtful thing but a shameful thing to make a prisoner of such a proud bird as a hawk, even a small hawk, an ordinary pigeon hawk such as this one, with his slate-gray back, his tawny breast streaked with brown. He carried his head erect above his square shoulders. His fierce dark eyes glanced through me as if I were a bug to be killed and eaten, nothing more. As a boy in Lothian I had learned falconry with such a hawk on my arm.

With the curved tip of his blue-black beak, and with his curved black claws, he plucked music from the bars of his prison.

I stood gazing with Gull by my side, and the harp notes flew up wild and free all around me—as a boy I had un-hooded hawks and watched them fly, free and hungry, and felt joy as keen as a knife in my chest. If the hawks would not come back to the lure I was glad, even though it meant a punishment for me; I flew my hawks badly so that they might fly away. I understood this harper hawk defying his cage with music, with notes that soared, golden, silver winged, singing *joy, happiness, freedom*. How brave of spirit he must be. I knew what it was to be a prisoner, trapped in despair. All creatures should be free, and fate should snip itself and die. If I had wings I would fly away.

As if he could hear me thinking, the hawk paused in his harping and looked at me.

He looked *at* me this time, not through me, his gaze as deep as a well. As never before I saw a falcon's nearly human eyes, dark as the dark of the moon between pallid yellow eyelids, under a frown of gray feathers. He opened his beak soundlessly. I saw his thick blue tongue, so very different from mine.

I took three steps, unlatched the door of the cage, and opened it wide.

A whir of pointed wings—he flew at once, as swiftly as only a falcon can fly. In an eye blink he darted above the treetops. With my head tilted back I watched as he circled once, then vanished eastward with a high, wild cry.

I lowered my gaze. "Well, Gull," I murmured, patting her.

I knew there would be a punishment.

But I smiled, for I knew I had done something good.

I looked around at twining plum trees, at snickering fountains, at tawny roses climbing to the sky, all golden in sunset light. Even without the music of the mystic harper, this was a garden of surpassing beauty. "Let's stay here tonight," I said to Gull. I sat down on the soft turf and patted my faithful brachet and watched her grin and pant in reply. I pressed my nose to her wet nose and stared cross-eyed at her. She licked me under the chin and I grinned; I felt happy. Maybe that was the answer to my quest, just to do good and be happy. Maybe there was no need to go on looking for Merlin.

In the morning it was all gone.

Roses, gone. Fruit trees interlaced into pavilions roofed in living leaves, gone. The golden spiral cage upon which the hawk had made harp music, gone. Fountains, hedges, yew trees shaped like peacocks, all gone. Even the tors with their muttering and their tottering crags, even the tittering forest—gone. Awakening, I blinked, and sat up and blinked again; I lay within a great hulking circle of standing stones—all that remained of the garden wall—on a wide, windy plain.

My sense of happiness, gone. The stones loomed, casting long shadows on me.

"Gull, come on." I got up, in a hurry to be away from that uncanny place, and went to catch the horse and saddle it and arm myself to ride. Gull trotted after me, cheerful as ever, her white wag of a tail merry in the air.

I had just buckled the breast harness to the saddle, and was turning to reach for the bridle, when I saw Gull fall.

Struck down by an invisible blow.

Her head snapped up as her back collapsed. Her mouth opened as if to cry out, but she made no sound. She thudded to the ground.

I ran to her. Still alive but dying, she looked up at me with stricken eyes. I dropped to my knees beside her and cupped her head in my hands. "Gull, what . . ." But my voice came out a puppyish whimper as I stared. She was broken, her back and neck shattered like a dove when the peregrine drops upon it and strikes it like a gauntleted fist out of the sky.

"Gull?" I whispered, bewildered. She gazed back at me, her suffering eyes pooled as dark and deep as ladywater, and in them I saw. I saw the hawk black and silent against the high sky, flying away. I saw—I saw that it had struck hard, for I saw white feathers drifting down like snow. Then I saw the prey falling, its pointed wings strewn ungracefully in death.

The white falcon.

Dead.

Killed.

I saw Nyneve. Her hawk-red hair flying as her head snapped up. Her face like a white flower, haunted, as her mouth opened in a silent scream.

Then the sheen went out of Gull's eyes, and they turned blank and milky. She shuddered, then lay still.

I folded to the ground beside her, pounded the earth with my fist and wept.

I lifted her in my arms—her sturdy white body was still warm, but being touched did not hurt her, and I knew she was truly dead. Her head lolled and her eyes saw nothing. I held her against my chest, I, Mordred, a knight of the Round Table, weeping, and I did not care, I hugged her in my arms and cried. I sobbed until I felt sick and still I could not stop crying. When Gull's body stiffened into the shape of my embrace and grew cold, I gently laid her down, and I struggled up and found my sword. I thought of killing myself for the villain that I was, wantwit, accursed, fate's fool. It might be the only way I could defy fate, to kill myself. But instead of doing it, I used the sword to hack a hole in the ground near where Gull lay, within the circle of standing stones; they would mark the place. As if I were fighting the earth I smote it, weeping.

I hated everything, most of all myself. Fool. I had gotten her killed.

And . . .

I could not yet think of Nyneve. I had to do at least this one last thing right for Gull. I had to dig the grave deep. Deep enough so that nothing, sun's heat or frost heave or the rooting of scavengers, nothing would disturb her.

I hacked earth with my clumsy broadsword for hours. It was the worst use to which I had ever put a weapon, or perhaps the best. When at last I felt certain that the grave was deep enough, I laid down the sword, and stood gathering breath and courage for a moment, then knelt and lifted her for the last time and placed her in the ground. She lay curled in the gritty darkness as if in my arms. I did not want to cover her, but I had to do it, and—that sound, the pattering sound of dirt falling down on dead love, like dry rain falling—it has to be the worst sound in the world. It made me half blind with tears, so that I saw only a blur, whiteness being buried in shadow.

I placed the earth on her handful by gentle handful—it

took some time. When I had buried Gull, I mounded the earth atop her and sobbed for Nyneve.

Dead.

Fate has no heart.

I sat by Gull's grave in that desolate place as day slouched on toward evening and the shadows lengthened. My weeping ceased, but I sat there bone weary, too weary to move, feeling an invisible serpent wind tight, tighter around my throat, watching without seeing as the shadows of the monoliths closed around me.

Then I saw, atop a long shadow edging toward my foot, the shadow of the murderer.

I looked up. Perched on top of the standing stone, he was only a dark shape against the glare of the lowering sun. "If I had a bow and arrow, you would be dead," I told him.

Just an ordinary pigeon hawk, as I have said. A merlin.

Merlin.

And how I hated myself for having set him free.

With a hawk's chuckle he swooped down and landed on the ground, three feet from me, within my sword's reach, as if to dare me. *Try it,* he said, the words sounding inside my head.

My hand closed around my sword hilt so hard that my fist whitened and trembled, but I did not move.

Go ahead, Merlin said. *I have no human form anymore, no human powers. Only the powers of a hawk—to fly high and far, to see acutely, to strike hard.*

"You are speaking to me," I whispered between clenched teeth.

That is your power, that you can hear me. Not mine.

I hated him almost as much as I hated myself. And it seemed to me that perhaps he wished to die, having had his revenge upon Nyneve. But some stubbornness within me would not let me kill him. Just as it would not let me kill myself.

He stood there with his dark stare and his wrinkled blinking eyelids and his sooty mustache of feathers drooping around his beak, a paltry bird to have done such damage, shifting his wax-yellow feet in discomfort because he was not used to perching on the ground.

It's no use, Mordred, he told me. *You are who you are. Stop struggling against it.*

But—if it were not for him, for his prophecy—who would I be?

I said, my voice as gritty as Gull's grave, "I should kill you for what you have done to me."

He chuckled again, a pigeon hawk's shrill giggle, *ki-ki-ki.* He said, *As a favor—because you found me despite all the baffles Nyneve had put in the way, and because in the goodness of your heart you freed me—I will tell you what you want to know.*

I stared at him.

He said, *You came to find out your own fate, is it not so?*

I sat clutching my sword. I could not move or speak.

He told it to me anyway. He told me that I would live a few years more, and he told me the manner of my own death.

He told it to me dryly, in simple words, what would someday happen at a place called Glastonbury—but my stomach

156

heaved, for I saw it happening. I saw the sunset battlefield, the thousands of knights lying dead, or wounded and groaning. I saw the few left standing, one of them King Arthur—my heart turned to water at the sight of his noble face. I saw the traitor rush upon him with drawn sword—it was I, Mordred. I saw King Arthur catch him below the shield with his lance, running him through, and I saw Mordred so possessed by desperate hatred that he thrust himself up to the crosspiece of the lance and dealt King Arthur a blow with the sword that cut through the helmet and into the skull beneath. Then he—I—fell to the earth, stark dead and gruesome with blood. I scried it all in the darkness of Merlin's eyes.

The knowledge drove through me like the lance I would someday take in my gut. I knew it was a wound from which I might never heal.

I felt faint. I felt my innards crawling like a nest of vipers. "Go away," I begged.

He clacked his beak at me, and chuckled once more, then flew—I did not see where, nor did I care. I lay on the ground, my face in the dirt, and I thought I would vomit but I did not, and I thought I would weep but I could not; all the tears had turned to stone in me.

I lay there through the night, with no white shadow beside me any longer. The wind moaned across the face of the empty world.

In the morning I struggled up, got on my horse and rode back toward Camelot. My quest was over.

BOOK FOUR

The Raven

14

ON MY KNEES BEFORE KING ARTHUR, I BEGGED, "HEAL me."

"Mordred, lad." His voice faltered with surprise. "What has happened?"

I looked up at him where he sat in his place at the rim of the Round Table. I looked into his sea-gray eyes, wise, regal, goodly, fierce, and fair, at his rugged face, so proud—yet for all his kingly pride, he did not hesitate to care for me. His gray gaze misted with worry. He knew the prophecy, yet he could feel for me? Yearning choked me; I could not speak.

He studied me. "You're wounded," he said, "and weary." It was true, for it had taken me hard weeks to fight my way back to Camelot; I had ventured farther away from my sire's court than I had thought. "Is that it? Come, do not kneel there; rise. You are a knight of the Round Table." He gestured for me to sit next to him. "Go from us," he told the servants and courtiers who were in the great hall, and they went silently away and left us alone. King Arthur turned his grave gaze to me. "Mordred, what is your need of healing? Tell me."

But how could I explain to him? I could tell him that my fishermother was dead or that Nyneve was dead or that Gull lay dead and buried, without beginning to delve the depth of my despair. I could tell him that I was defeated, that my quest had failed—but he knew that already just from looking at me. I could tell him—but I could not tell him that I needed to be his son truly, that the fate coiled like a serpent around me, always whispering in my ear. To say anything more would have been treason.

"You know why I am sick at heart," I said harshly, "as well as I do." This was not quite true; I probably knew more of his own death, by that time, than he did.

He sat silently, his gray gaze awash with trouble. Then he lifted his hands, reached through the small distance between us and laid his palms on my hair, cupping my head between his hands. It was the first time he had touched me, except with his sword the day he knighted me.

His touch felt warm, that was all. If my pain had not been so great, his warm touch might have comforted me—but that was all. I felt no power of healing in him.

"Mordred?" he whispered.

I pulled back and looked at him. I remember that he wore the clothing of an ordinary yeoman—a plain russet tunic with a leather belt, brown breeches, brown boots—yet no one could have mistaken him for other than the King.

He saw in my eyes the answer to his barely spoken question. He laid his hands on the table and breathed out a long breath that might have been a sigh. "I cannot heal you," he said, his voice low but steady now, as befitted a King. "I can not heal those whom I—" Whatever he had been about to say, he stopped short of it. He turned his hands palm up and looked at them as if they were strangers. He had fair hands, I remember, large knuckled and strong with no blemishes on them. "Like Guinevere," he said quietly. "She is my own beloved wife, and I cannot help her."

"Why is that?" I asked just as quietly.

He looked at me, bleak. "I have done wrong. I must accept my punishment."

Anger jolted me to my feet so suddenly that I overturned my chair. "But what have *I* done?" I cried at him. I did not wait for an answer, for there was no answer. I bowed, giving him barest courtesy, and then I left him.

That was a dark winter.

I spent it mostly in the kennel, lying in the straw with Gull's puppies—full-grown brachets and brach-hounds now. Three spotted, one black; the three white ones had died. Any one of the four that survived would give me a nudge with a wet nose or a lick with a pink tongue, but none of them was Gull. Still, they were of some comfort to me.

I would not stay in the empty tower that waited for Nyneve and Pelleas to return. I found myself a chamber in the basement of the keep—a dank, shadowy place; it suited my mood.

Sometimes Gawain and Garet visited me there or in the

kennel. They had heard that I was a fighter now, or they could see it in me, and they were friendly to me, even kind. They never spoke of Tintagel. And I knew that I should forgive them; what they had done—killing Pellinore, killing Morgause and Lamorak—it was no more than what was needful to defend their honor. Folk looked up to them, for they were knights of the Round Table and, yes, there was still that glow about them that had awed me when I first came to Camelot. But now I could not look at them without feeling my gut crawl.

They had done such bloody deeds.

I could not sleep at night. When I did sleep, my black dreams would show to me again what Merlin had showed me, the bloody deed I must do someday, and I would awaken in a cold sweat.

Evil. I could no longer doubt that I was fated to do evil.

I took to wearing black clothing. It suited my mood and made damsels turn their heads and look at me, though they shied away. Other than that, I did not think why I chose to dress in black; I wore it on a dark whim. I did not know then that I would be wearing black for eternity.

On a similar whim, I cut my hair to show what I had always hidden: the blemish behind my ear, the birthmark I had never seen. A mark like a ragged X, my mother, Morgause, had said. But Nyneve had called it a dark bird flying.

I hated myself.

I have only a few good memories of those shadowed days:

The white, aspiring ramparts of Camelot. On a rare day of winter sunshine I looked up at them and knew with a pang that I belonged there. It was a castle under a spell, as I have said, and it had taken me back. I belonged there, fate and all.

Pellinore's son, Sir Torre, saying to me, "You know, Mordred, you are not to blame." I thought he meant for his father's death and his brother's death, but he said, "We bastards are not to blame for any of it."

Garet, asking me, "Do you grieve for our mother?" And meaning it, even though it was he who had seized her by the hair and beheaded her.

Gawain, telling me, "I was always jealous of you for the sake of that brachet of yours. She would follow you anywhere. No dog was ever so faithful to me. No woman either."

King Arthur's smile as he offered me yet another gift. "Mordred, lad, I'd like to have a proper shield made for you. What device shall we put on it?" And I did not know how to answer him.

Pelleas riding in, worn so thin that sunlight seemed to shine through him, as if he were an angel. He had achieved the quest of the Grail—one of only four knights ever to do so, the others being Bors, Percival, and that bastard virgin Sir Galahad. Pelleas did not know me. He knew no one but King Arthur.

It was Pelleas who gave me my solution, in a way.

I went to see him in the tower he had once shared with Nyneve. Servants looked after him there, for he would not have eaten if they had not fed him. He was transfigured, folk said.

It clenched my heart to see him sitting there so thin and

pale, with no white falcon on his shoulder, yet alight with happiness as he stared through the windows, up at the empty sky.

"Pelleas?"

He did not turn to me until I spoke his name. Then he gave me the same smile he gave everyone, as if he carried a sunrise inside him.

"Pelleas—" I wanted to get my errand over with quickly. "Pelleas, did they tell you about Nyneve?"

He did not answer. His smile shone yet warmer as he stared at me. "You were there," he said.

"Yes." I swallowed hard and sat down across from him. "Well, no." In a way I had not been there when Nyneve died. I wondered often whether she knew beforehand what I was doing, whether she knew I was to blame. Whether she hated me. "I saw her—"

"You were there. I saw your reflection in the silver chalice." Pelleas leaned toward me. "What is your name?"

"I—" I was a fool. I could not tell him my name; his sun-lit innocence would not let me. I could not tell him about Nyneve either.

He didn't care. He rushed on. "Did you touch it? Did you touch the Grail?"

"I—no. Did you?"

"No. I only saw. Oh, so beautiful." His rapt gaze wandered back to the sky.

"What did it show you?" Somehow, once upon a time, the mere sight of the Grail in a vision had brought forth all that was brave and good and pure in me. My dream of the Grail had made a knight of me and given to me my quest. But

166

somehow, since the quest had failed, I could not think what I had seen in the Grail except for blood.

"Why—I'm not sure." He focused on me for a moment, puzzled yet unclouded. "It was glorious, that's all. You were there. And I saw—" His head lifted. His sunrise smile widened. His hands drifted up like leaves on a breeze, like wings. "I saw my soul fly up."

"Your . . . your soul?"

"Like a white butterfly." His arms spread, but not as if he were showing me; he seemed no longer aware of me at all. He looked to the sky.

I said softly, "My soul is more like a moth that's been through the fire." Tattered, blackened, beaten down by fate. Barely alive.

I left Pelleas. He did not see me go.

From time to time throughout the dark winter days, I thought of him as my sluggish, miserable battle ground on, as the invisible serpent around me coiled tighter, as I felt a tiny, struggling self fluttering more and more weakly in my chest.

Slowly I came to shape a desperate plan.

Spring came, but it made no difference to me. I had hoped I would feel better when the grass turned green again, but I did not. I was soul weary and suffering. Birdsong and violets could not help me.

With spring, the blind harper came back to Camelot.

It seemed that nothing could stop my pain; each day I felt more tormented. But I wondered whether the blind harper might help me. Although I had reason to be wary of harping, something in his music spoke to me. And his harp—it was richly carved with druid vine work, very old. I sensed that this blind bard might see more clearly than people with eyes.

As I walked out one morning, there he sat in the sun of the courtyard, all alone except for the raven on his shoulder. Strumming his harp, he sang to the bird with bleak affection in his voice:

> *Three ravens sat on a tree*
> *And they were black as destiny.*
> *One of them said to his mate,*
> *"I'm hungry. What is there to eat?"*
> *"On Glastonbury field," she said,*
> *"Many and many a knight lies dead . . ."*

Somehow it did not surprise me that he knew what was to happen on Glastonbury field. But I did not wish to hear his song of it. "Harper!" I strode up to him. He halted his song and lowered his harp.

"Pretty boy," the raven greeted me.

I ignored it. "Do you know who I am?" I challenged the harper.

He replied without hesitation. "You are one who wears black."

"Do you know why?"

"You grieve because you know how the song must end." His milky eyes stared straight ahead. As if he did not care whether he angered me, he said, "You are a fool to be troubled. Do you not know that all songs must end? Waves crest,

168

then break themselves on the sand. Kings reign in glory, then die. There is no beauty in anything without ending."

"Scant comfort," I muttered.

He said nothing, only strummed at his harp, as if it could speak for him. I sat next to him on white stone and tried to take more comfort from the music than I had from his words. But I had heard the music of the harpers of Avalon. I had heard the harping of a merlin in a magical cage. This wanderer's harping sounded like the wind in sere grass by comparison.

I said to him, "I have given up trying to change the song's ending. But I would like to save what is left of my soul." The poor, defeated thing.

"See a holy man."

"No. I mean really save it, put it in safekeeping, as the druids used to do for heroes venturing into the realms of the dead. Or so the old tales say."

His fingers stopped twiddling at his harp strings and he grew very still. The raven sat on his shoulder, making small croaking noises deep in its black-feathered throat.

"You are of druid blood," I guessed.

"Yes."

"Will you help me?"

"Why should I?"

"Gold. I can pay you well." With gifts King Arthur had given me.

He nodded. Then he said something odd, considering that he had showed no human warmth so far. "Do you trust me?"

"Why should I?"

"Do you trust anyone?"

No, my silence said, I scarcely trusted anyone.

"Your soul must be given to someone whom you trust," the harper told me, "or it cannot be given at all."

"Let me think," I muttered, and I got up and left him sitting there.

"Oddling," the raven accused my back as I walked away.

I walked alone, as the raven had known I must.

Whom could I trust? Friends? I had none. Sweetheart? Ha. My brothers? Hardly. Nyneve—yes, I had trusted her, but she was dead. Sometimes I felt like she was only away from me, riding through the Forest Perilous on a dapple-gray charger, I forgot that she was dead, and then when I remembered, I felt the pain of her dying all over again. Dead, like my mother whom my brothers had killed. Like my—

No. My father was not dead.

My—father . . .

The King.

King Arthur.

How strange—but yes, yes, I trusted him utterly.

> *Hark to what the cuckoo's saying:*
> *Shy in the valley the violets grow,*
> *Bold in the meadow the buttercups glow,*
> *Time to go a-Maying!*

It's a sweet song, and sweetly the lords and ladies sang it as they rode out on their many-colored pleasure horses that May Day. But I did not ride with them. I had no lady for whom to gather violets and buttercups, and my thoughts were dark, and I wore a black velvet tunic, black leggings, and black boots, not springtime finery. I rode out, but on one of King Arthur's hot-blooded black colts, not on a pleasure pony. And I rode a different path.

King Arthur had ridden out early that morning, as always on May Day, alone and somber. I did not follow him; no one dared to follow him. But now I rode to where a fey instinct, almost a dream, had told me I might find him.

I rode down the same cart trail that had taken me southward more than a year ago, with Gull flitting like a white butterfly at my side, on the first day of my quest. Remembering that bright-eyed young knight, Mordred, was like remembering a friend who had died.

Today I wore no helm, no mail, no shield, and no weapons, not even a dagger at my belt. If someone tried to kill me, good. More power to him.

But no one challenged me as I followed the rude road down to the sea.

It was blessedly as I remembered it. The salt tang in the air. The coarse grass where curlews flew. The half circle of rocks forming a cove. The gravel shore. The quay where a coracle waited, cradled on the waves.

And beyond it all, the vastness of the sea, which had tried to kill me, and which I loved.

And sitting on the rocks, gazing out on the gray water with his gray visionary eyes, my other enemy whom I loved.

He did not turn to look at me, though he must have heard the ringing of my colt's hooves on the stone. I dismounted, hobbled the horse to let it wander in the salty grass, and went to sit beside him.

He turned his head to me just for a moment, then turned back to gazing on the gray, endless washing of the sea. "Mordred," he said quietly, "it is your birthday. My very best wishes. Long life and much happiness to you."

As happened so often when I was with him, his goodness surprised me so that I could not speak. I watched a chalk-gray sea hawk fly and said nothing. Likely he thought I was sullen.

"Seventeen years," said King Arthur, his voice very low.

Seventeen years of May Days he had been coming here. Last year, for my sixteenth birthday, where had I been? Questing for a way to save us both.

The quest had failed.

"Sire," I said, "I would beg an audience with you."

My formality amused him, for I had given him not so much as a bow until now, and there we sat side by side on rocks splashed with gull dung; even in his bleak mood the King kept a sense of the droll. He turned to me with merriment in his eyes. "You have my whole attention, Mordred."

I hated to take that silver glint of laughter from his eyes. I looked at my own hands, not at him, as I spoke.

"Sire," I said, "I am seventeen now, and I will be twenty-seven when I die." It was a knowledge so cold that I felt as if I had dreamed it, but I knew it was no dream; the hawk had told me. "I have ten years left to live before—before the day Merlin prophesied."

I think I took his breath away. He knew his own doom,

but he did not know the time of it, and he did not know mine. "You . . . you speak of—"

"The final battle. I will die also." This came perilously close to saying what was never to be uttered. Or not by me. But he did not flinch.

"How do you know this?"

"I have spoken with Merlin."

He stood up to study me, but I stayed sitting where I was. His gaze upon me forced me to look at him, and I peered up, blinking, like a child; he could see that I did not threaten him. He said slowly, "If this is so—"

"*If*, Sire? But you know Merlin speaks true." I was worn down with the wretchedness of hating what I was destined to do, and I let him see my misery. I rose to stand facing him; I lifted my hands to him, pleading. "Why have you not killed me already? Why do you not do it now, this very moment? One sword thrust, and it would be over."

He could not look at me. He turned to the sea, and stared out over the waves, and he said, very low, "I was heartsick, last time. I did not want to live my life at such a price. Then I was glad despite all reason when I heard that you had survived."

Close. He came so close to saying it.

He walked along the stony shore, and I walked with him, the chill, salt sea wind hissing in my ears. We walked in silence, side by side, with the unspeakable truth hovering on the windy space between us, until I could not bear that haunted silence any longer and broke it.

"My King, it is not death that I fear," I told him. "But

until death comes, it is hard for me to be who I am." I waited for King Arthur's reply. He gave me none. "Sire," I said, "when I first came to Camelot, you offered me a boon. I will claim it now."

His voice as harsh as the gravel, he said, "Do not ask me to kill you in cold blood."

"No, Sire. There is a span of life left to me, and I am not so willing to throw it away. But neither do I wish to spend it suffering." I stood still, and he stopped his pacing and faced me, and I described to him what I wanted him to do.

He was so aghast that his gray eyes winced and his face paled behind the proud tilt of his beard. "Sir Mordred," he protested.

"Sire, I charge you by your promised boon to do this thing. It is because of you that I find myself born to be in constant pain."

We stood staring at each other. Perhaps as he stood there by the sea he saw in me something of himself. I would like to think so.

"Sire," I urged.

"You are mortally certain that this fearsome thing is what you wish?"

"Yes."

"Then I must do as you say."

15

WE HAD TO WAIT FOR SEVERAL DAYS, UNTIL THE MOON had waned and the time came for doing mystic acts. Then on that night, the night of the dark of the moon, we had to wait until innocents were asleep. Long after dark, after midnight, on a night when not even stars shed light, we met in the courtyard. King Arthur commanded the guards to open the gates, and we slipped out—on foot, for the blind harper was too old and frail to ride—walking in silence.

Over the wide sweep of the meadows, night hung silent; the summer crickets had not yet begun to speak. Only an owl spoke sometimes from the forest.

We walked until the white towers of Camelot rose far behind us and we could no longer see them in the darkness. It took perhaps an hour, because the blind harper walked slowly. On the farthest rise of the meadow, near the Forest Perilous, we stopped and faced each other. It was just the three of us: King Arthur and I and the blind harper with the raven riding on his shoulder, black and invisible in the moonless night.

"Mordred," my sire asked me one more time, "are you sure?"

"Yes."

"It is not too late to turn back."

"I am certain, my liege." *My father.* Because emotion was closing my throat, I sounded surly.

The harper had explained to me what I must do, and I did it quickly to prevent any more talk. I unlaced my tunic to bare myself. I stood facing the east, facing the forest, with my arms spread wide so as to unlock my chest—thin, I had grown so thin I felt my ribs ridging my skin. I stood with my hands straining back while the harper chalked the mystic circle around all three of us for protection from the spirits of the night. Night is perilous always, but we would be especially at its mercy while the spell made us vulnerable, while he opened me.

He anointed my face and my bared chest and outflung wrists with pungent oil, his blind hands fumbling at me so that I shuddered.

King Arthur stood facing me. "Mordred," he whispered, the single word, my name.

I did not answer.

The blind harper took his place and struck his harp, chanting strange words in the druidic tongue.

King Arthur lifted his hands to his heart, cupping between them the casket, the small silk-lined coffer of pure gold in which he would receive whatever might fly from my chest.

If I had to take my soul out of my body and give it to someone for safekeeping . . .

It had to be someone whom I trusted.

He waited.

It did not take long. It was far easier than I expected, far easier than it would have been for anyone less worn and alone than I. Without even a need to say good-bye I felt it leave me, I felt it fly, I felt self take wing. Before, there had been the slow constant ache of my struggle with fate. As soul took flight, there was a sharper pang, as if my thin, taut body were a harp string, plucked. Then there was a simple, welcome nothingness, a soundless peace, and near my face I saw the white moth fluttering in the night.

King Arthur awaited it with a pale face but steady hands to cherish it for my sake. Though to tell the truth, once I was rid of the troublesome thing I no longer cared whether he cherished it or not. I let my arms fall to my sides. The stillness within me welled deep, so deep I could float on it, as if on the lake of Avalon. All was peaceful and silent and floating, like water lilies. Nothing mattered to me. Nothing.

Dancing on the dark air went my soul, no larger than a dandelion puff, hardly as substantial as cloud wisp.

With relief as vast as the sea, I watched it go. But then— before it reached my liege, I heard a harsh noise I did not at first recognize, and a clacking sound. And it was gone.

My white wisp of soul. Gone.

The raven!

I had given the bird no thought until it sounded its triumphant croak and lunged, black and unseen in the moonless night, and snapped up the tiny white thing in its doomster bill. I heard its wings rustle like black storm wind rising as it flew away. And I heard its throaty laughter, and the hoarse words it flung back at me: "Mordred! More dread, more dead, murderer, Mordred!"

King Arthur let the golden casket clatter to the ground as he leaped toward the harper, roaring, "Is this your doing, villain?" He reached for his sword.

But the harper was gone like a puff of black smoke in the night, as if he were a—I do not like to say it. Perhaps he was merely a prudent man fleeing the King's wrath, a blind man moving more quickly than we sighted ones in the dark. I do not know what he was, for I never saw him or heard news of him again.

In silence the King and I found our way back to Camelot.

When we reached the white ramparts, King Arthur led me through the gatehouse and across outer ward and inner ward to the keep, where we entered the great hall. No folk were about, for it was the hour when even the owls are silent. The Round Table stood great and shadowy like an odd sort of monument, a circle hewn of stone, in the night.

King Arthur took a candle from a sconce on the wall and crouched to light it from an ember in the hearth. When it wavered into yellow flame he arose, lifted it, and looked at me.

"Mordred?" he asked, very low.

"I am grateful," I told him, and those were the last sincere words I spoke to him. Already I felt the old, childish hatred stirring in my marrow—now unopposed. No longer would the struggle between fate and soul disturb my sleep. "The pain is gone."

"Yes," he said, grim, "and so is the light in your eyes."

"It was never of any use to me."

"I had hoped to give your soul back to you someday, some way."

"It does not matter, Sire. I thank you." My thanks were bland. I would be able now to watch and wait and eat heartily at his table—and betray him when it was time. "Nothing matters. Let my soul fly where it will."

He looked at me for a moment longer, his lips pressed together in a flat, shadowed line. Then he bowed his head and blew out the candle.

That night, or what was left of it, I slept at once, deeply, peacefully, without a dream.

When I awoke, in the middle of the next day, and when I had eaten, I went to find Gawain and Garet. I found them on the practice field and sparred with them and jested with them easily. No longer did I feel any horror of them. On the way back to the keep, I met a damsel, and I smiled at her and spoke to her, for I felt no shame anymore. The damsel looked at me uncertainly but returned my greeting.

I climbed the spiral stairway to where Pelleas sat in the top of his tower peering up at the sky. "She's dead, you know," I told him.

He turned to me eyes like mirrors, bright and blank. "What?"

"She's dead."

"Who?"

"Nyneve."

His rapture never wavered. His shining eyes did not cloud. "Who?"

"Your wife. She's dead."

"Wife?"

If he did not remember her, who would? Not I. I shrugged. "May I move in? Down below? You're not using those rooms, are you?"

When I had summoned servants and set them to moving my things out of my dark basement chamber and into Nyneve's comfortable tower, there was still a little time before supper. I wandered to the kennel. There were four fine young brach-hounds and brachets in there, three spotted and one pure black, like the black hounds I had seen somewhere once chasing some kind of a white deer. Happy young dogs. But when I walked in, they looked at me and trembled and cringed with their tails under them. They whimpered and ran away.

Epilogue

Because he was the True King, he was therefore the most helpless of men. He had to follow where fate and honor led, or the skies would burn. He had done wrong, and he had to take his punishment, or the rain would turn to poison. He had to let it all happen, or the fields would blacken and grow only stone.

When Sir Mordred accused Queen Guinevere of treason with Sir Lancelot, the True King had to sentence her to burn at the stake.

When Sir Lancelot rescued her and became an enemy, the True King had to fight him.

And when Sir Mordred took the opportunity to make a bid for the throne, the True King had to strike him down.

Thus it had all led to this fateful day and this final battlefield.

Sundown. King Arthur stood bloodied and so heartsick that he wept. Dead, dead, they all lay dead, Gawain these three days in his grave, Garet killed by Lancelot, and every remaining knight of the Round Table, the flower of all knighthood, the jeweled crown of all knighthood, they all lay dead or painfully dying on the trampled grass. No one remained horsed, and only four remained standing: Arthur himself, Sir Lucas, and Sir Bedivere, and—staggering toward them like a shadow out of the sunset, all in black armor, carrying a black shield, running at them with lifted sword— Sir Mordred, he who would have called himself King.

A worthy foe. He had fought mightily. King Arthur felt almost proud of him.

A different sort of pride made him harden his face and stop his tears.

Swooping low in the golden light over the battlefield there flew a great bird on black wings that rustled like a rising wind. King Arthur barely noticed. Many ravens had gathered over the battlefield, feasting.

It was time.

"Sir Mordred," he challenged, "defend yourself!"

He lifted his lance in his hand and ran, tottering with weariness and the weight of his armor, at his son, his enemy, Mordred, rushing to meet him.

He aimed well. His long weapon caught Mordred in the belly just below the black shield, and the force of King Arthur's attack and the force of Mordred's own charge drove the lance through Mordred's armor and mail, deep, a mortal wound. It should have been over then. But such was the courage of the lad, or the fire of his hatred, or the power of fate, that Mordred welcomed the wound and ran up the shaft of the lance, brandishing his sword with both hands, and struck—then fell dead.

And the raven flew low over them both, laughing its croaking laugh.

Arthur remembered little, then, until Sir Lucas and Sir Bedivere brought him to Avalon.

Odd: That old trickster Merlin had lied after all. He was supposed to be dead, but he had not died. The wound Mordred had given him to his head was severe; he would need to rest and heal for a long time—maybe hundreds of years—but he was not dead.

King Arthur awoke in an airy pavilion alight with the white scent of water lilies. He felt no pain, only a great, lazy ease. For a moment he drifted on a wisp of dream, something about floating in a bright, still pool, amid blue swans—but no, he lay in a white bed canopied with gossamer, his wounded head upon a white pillow, and he looked into the smiling face of a lady he remembered: Vivien, she who had given him Excalibur.

"Rest," she told him, smoothing his hair back from his forehead with one petal-soft hand; the touch of her hand sent peace rippling through him. "Sleep."

But his glance wandered beyond her, to the railing of the pavilion, where asphodel grew. Above the white blossoms perched a shining black bird.

Vivien turned to see at what he looked, and the sadness that tinged her smile only made it more sweet. She said, "There he is, once again at one with his soul." She turned to the King and said, "He will guard your sleep and await your wakening. He will live for as long as you need him."

Arthur gazed at the raven, his gray eyes widening. "Mordred?" he murmured.

The raven lifted its wings and glided to the foot of his bed. In the harsh croak of a bird it spoke a single word. "Father."

The King's eyes filled with tears. The King wept. "Mordred," he said. "Mordred, my son."